STORY

FANTAIL

Fantail Publishing
An Imprint of Puffin Enterprises

Published by the Penguin Group
27 Wrights Lane, London W8 5TZ

First published by Fantail Publishing, 1989

0140 901531

10 9 8 7 6 5 4 3 2 1

Made and printed in Great Britain by
Richard Clay Ltd, Bungay, Suffolk

prologue

'Hold it Susan ... Hey, that's just beautiful honey! Show me that gorgeous smile! ... And now a left profile. Now laugh sweetie! Remember, this perfume's the fragrance to set you free ... Throw your head back ... come on ... dazzle me ... You know you look stunning ... and you want to make all those women green with envy ...'

The photographer's voice was now just a drone, a monotone inside Susan Morris's head. Another click. Another smile. The hot lights beat down on her and she suddenly felt too exposed by their intense penetration; indignant at their intrusion. Modelling was second nature to her but today was the first time she could remember feeling the need to run away from the lights, from the cameras that saw too much, from the false compliments of the 'genius' now giving her directions. A drop of perspiration which had been forming at the base of her neck now began its journey down her back.

'OK ... Susan ... now really turn it on. I am coming in for the close ups!' She gulped in a quick breath of air remembering the puffy, swollen eyes she'd looked at in the mirror that morning. Click! Click!

'Think about how you want to splash this perfume all over you and run out to meet the man of your dreams.' The lights became suddenly hotter.

'Run out!' Susan thought wearily with an inward shudder. 'God – she was nine months pregnant and she felt like death. Or hadn't this 'genius' noticed? And as for the man of her dreams – Who? – George?' But she smiled, turned, swayed to the music which was always a part of these Studio sessions. She preened. She posed. And all the while, through the glare of the lights, she could see George, her husband, pacing back and forth behind the cameras carrying what she observed to be the mandatory cup of coffee. That coffee cup, always in his hand, during her photographic shoots, was like his stage prop – something he held on to, just like he'd held on to her all these years.

'Escape' was the new perfume range being launched by George Morris's Advertising Agency. It would be just the product to keep

Susan in the limelight while she was off giving birth to this baby she'd been so determined to keep, he'd decided. If he kept it to 'head and shoulders' shots only, it would be the perfect assignment to provide her transition from the glamorous 'mum-to-be' category which she'd been working in for the past six months, back into mainstream modelling. He was happy with the success of his push to promote her as Australia's most fashionable 'mother-to-be', especially when her pregnancy was not something he'd planned on. Her appearance on the covers of all the best women's magazines had consoled him. But now it was time to think about the future. Susan had come a long way since that first day she'd arrived at his office as a substitute Secretary. He wasn't about to let a baby, even his baby, undermine all the hard work he'd put in. He'd moulded Susan from the little hick suburban nothing she was back than into the highly successful fashion model he now watched promoting his Company's new perfume contract. Her beauty still took his breath away, even now in what he saw as her rotund and disfigured condition of pregnancy. And he still had plans for Susan. She'd reached the pinnacle of Australian modelling, but now he could see the potential in the overseas market.

New York was where the money was. Give her three, maybe four weeks after the birth, and then he could start negotiations. George slurped his coffee and grimaced, finding it had gone cold. He glanced at his watch. This shoot looked like finishing late and he had interviews lined up back at the Agency. Prospective nannies were his current priority. He'd lay down the law to Susan: a nanny would be on hand to handle all the rearing the child would demand. That way Susan could concentrate on getting herself back into shape and, within the month, they should be able to leave all this worry behind them.

Susan felt a wave of nausea sweep over her, but she put it down to the intense studio lights. 'This squeamish feeling is something you learn to live with during pregnancy,' she told herself. Even when she was going through those first horrific morning-sickness periods, she was glad, knowing it meant her baby was still growing inside her. George had been furious when she had announced she was going to have a baby. He demanded that she seek an abortion. All he could think about was her career. But she stood her ground. She had wanted this baby right from the start. Planned on it, without telling

George, knowing he would disapprove. But eventually, George had even started to warm to the idea of 'his' child coming into the world. Perhaps a baby might be the only true worth to come from their marriage. Looking back she was sure now that marrying George had been the major mistake of her life. He had never really treated her as his wife but more like one of his possessions. He was her agent and marrying her had merely extended their contract to a life-long term. And she had never 'loved' him. Not the way she dreamed 'love' could be. Even back then she'd felt something was missing. But, she'd married George because he'd proposed to her and she was used to following his instructions. And she'd owed him so much. Or so she'd thought back then. The first pain hit her as they set up for 'the wind in the hair' shots. Susan had never before experienced a physical pain like it. She slumped to the ground.

'Susan baby – what's happening?' the photographer shrieked.

George was bending over his wife, concern written all over his face. For a moment, she thought she glimpsed genuine love in his eyes.

'Do you think you can finish this shoot, Susan? There's a lot riding on this you know.' George's voice was gruff and business-like and Susan's vision of love disintegrated. The pain was beginning to ease and George helped her up.

'That's my girl,' he said, condescendingly, and she felt a surge of hatred rise within her. 'Just three more shots!' he urged.

As strategically placed fans blew her hair into the fresh and free-look needed, the cameras clicked on.

'Beautiful, beautiful! OK sweetie, that's it! We've got enough for now,' the 'genius' behind the cameras announced, as the second pain jabbed at Susan's body, more severe than the first.

George quickly stepped into his proud father-to-be role as he rushed Susan to the car, calling for help from the studio crew. He insisted on driving her to the Hospital himself, knowing that this would look best and would fit the image he hoped to achieve.

As they pulled up at the Hospital, he was pleased to see the Press waiting by the main doors. His message, sent through that idiot photographer, had apparently been received. Susan, on the other hand, was horrified. 'I can't think who could have alerted them,' George lied to his wife as he bustled her through the clicking lenses, feigning irritation with the barrage of questions being hurled at them.

'I'm sorry, ladies and gentlemen,' George announced from the doors with a theatrical flourish of his hand. 'But my wife is in labour and we're about to have our baby now. I will talk to you all later.'

Susan couldn't believe it. George had even managed to turn her labour into a fashion shoot. 'Click, click' went the cameras again before she could gain sanctuary within the Hospital's interior. Despite his denial, she knew he was behind the Press being there. Would there ever be a part of her life which he didn't control? But she couldn't think any longer. The pains were coming closer together now. Soon she would have her baby.

All through the labour, George remained in the Delivery Room. Susan's pain was intense and she gained no relief from the presence of her husband. Every time she looked up at his masked face, she saw only her Agent waiting impatiently for her to be ready for her next assignment.

'A girl,' the Doctor finally announced. 'A beautiful baby girl.' Susan began to cry with joy as the baby was placed in her arms.

'My little Samantha,' George said tenderly looking over his wife's shoulder, admiring his baby daughter. But Susan was still gripped by pain and the need to bear down.'

'It's going to be twins,' the Doctor suddenly announced with surprise. A second baby was placed in Susan's arms not long after.

'A twin sister for your little Samantha, Mr Morris,' the nurse said. But George suddenly erupted, exposing his true nature.

'Damn you Susan,' he accused his wife, 'we don't need a second brat!' George's voice echoed through the Delivery Room as his angry hostile figure strode out, leaving his wife and twin daughters alone with the medical staff. A smile spread across Susan's face as she gazed down at her second baby.

'Finally, something of me he couldn't control,' Susan said aloud.

'What are you going to call this little one?' the Nurse asked sympathetically.

'I'll name her after my mother,' Susan said with pride. 'I wanted it all along but my husband insisted upon "Samantha". It looks like we can both have our way now.'

'What name's that dear?' the Nurse asked wiping Susan's forehead.

'Carly. This is my daughter Carly,' Susan announced proudly.

Carly Morris lay next to her twin sister in her mother's arms, little knowing of the pain and rejection that awaited her in life.

chapter one

George Morris waited impatiently as the auditorium began to fill. He was pleased to see the Press had come out in such numbers. Word had obviously spread about Susan's modelling success in Europe and the States. But where the hell was that blasted Davis woman? If the twins didn't arrive soon, his planned publicity stunt wouldn't come off.

He glanced towards the back of the hall. One of the woman journos caught his eye and waved. He nodded, endeavouring to cover his mounting anxiety. It had been five years since Susan had modelled in Australia. Right after the twins had been born, he'd bagged that assignment in New York. From then on it had all been smooth sailing. Success after success. America and then Europe. But it was important to show them all back here that his protégé was still number one. And to do that he needed the Press. The twins would be just the ticket to get those hard-

nosed journos back on his side. Their gim-
mick value was enormous. He'd never before
allowed his daughters to see Susan at work.
Their own natural excitement at the prospect
would lend a great human-interest angle to
a story on Susan's return. Instead of fashion
page snippets, maybe a feature article would
be written. Of course, all this depended upon
that new Nanny arriving with the twins on
time. George glanced quickly to the back of
the hall again and was swamped with relief
as he saw his daughters appear. 'Finally,'
he moaned inwardly.

'Straight down to the front, the pair of you,'
a woman, with a slightly nasal voice, instructed the two small girls beside her.

'Yes Nanny Davis,' Samantha answered
meekly, grabbing her twin sister, Carly, by
the hand and proceeding forward. But as
their Nanny turned to leave, Samantha spun
about and abruptly poked out her tongue at
the retreating figure.

'And don't you dob!' she warned Carly. 'Or
I'll chinese burn you, see!' She smiled an-
gelically at Carly, her appearance covering
the malice of her words. It was a paradox
Carly was now well used to. She knew that
smiles from either her sister or her father

didn't necessarily mean anything. The only smiles she was sure of were those of her mother.

Samantha pulled slightly at Carly's hand, urging her towards the beckoning figure of their father who waited in the front row. But suddenly their arrival had been noticed by the Press – just as George had planned it.

All at once, cameras began clicking and flashing as George rose to meet his daughters and the Press began to encircle the trio. Then his answers began to the questions being hurled from every direction.

'Yes, these are Susan's and my daughters ... identical twins, that's right.' George began to relax, feeling now everything was falling in place. He ever so subtly pushed Samantha to the front, knowing her charm and outgoing personality would have all these gossip mongers eating out of her hand in no time.

'Samantha was my first born,' George announced with an assumed fatherly pride as the flashing cameras centred on his favoured twin. The child preened and smiled, clearly enjoying the limelight.

'Yes, I think she is probably the one to have inherited her mother's talent,' George continued insensitively as the forgotten Carly receded to the side of the circle. The child felt grateful when she heard the fanfare rise, announcing the beginning of the parade and saw the Press again take their seats. At last she was going to see her mother on the catwalk.

She wriggled in her seat, excited by the prospect. But as she glanced at her father and Samantha, they both seemed still flushed with their own success with the Press, showing no interest at all in Susan's forthcoming appearance. Maybe that was the reason why she and Sam were allowed to come today, Carly decided. But she didn't care why she was here, just so long as she was. As the lights dimmed, Carly's small heart began to beat faster.

Susan appeared on the catwalk and the audience breathed a sigh of approval. Carly watched her mother her adoration. She saw none of the other models; only Susan was real to her. The figures on the catwalk swayed and moved rhythmically in time to the music now sweeping through the auditorium. But Carly's eyes followed only Susan's figure. And as her mother left the stage, Carly felt an overpowering need to be with her. She glanced at her father and sister through the semi-darkness, and noticed George's arm resting on Samantha's shoulder. They wouldn't even miss her if she slipped backstage to see her mother, she thought to herself as an impulse raised her from her seat.

Samantha watched Carly leave the auditorium with a narrowed gaze, knowing just where her twin sister would be headed. She always did run to their mother when things weren't going her way. Samantha glanced quickly at her father, noticing his ignorance of the situation. And as a black taffeta dress rippled above her, she decided to wait and let Carly really cause some trouble before blowing the whistle on her disappearing act.

Carly pushed her way through a door and was jostled as she attempted to wade through a sea of moving legs. Maybe this was a mistake after all! How was she going to find her mother in all this confusion? But the corridor suddenly cleared and she came upon a fresh-faced blond boy, not much taller than herself.

'Hello, you lookin' for someone?' the boy asked as he bounced a small rubber ball on the wall.

'My mother,' Carly replied shyly.

'Oh ... well ... if she's a model ... my father probably knows her. My father's Norman Peterson, Australia's top fashion photographer,' the boy announced parrot-fashion to Carly. This boy was certainly good at catching the ball, she noticed, as he hadn't missed a single catch yet. 'And I'm Derek,' he continued. 'What's your name?'

'Carly Morris,' she said. 'My mother is Susan.'

'Susan Morris?' Derek shrieked as Carly nodded proudly. 'My Dad thinks she's terrific. He has taken heaps of photos of her. Here, do you want to try,' Derek said, handing her the ball and taking Carly by surprise.

'Oh, no thanks. I've got to find my mother,' Carly said, giving the ball back.

'OK. Suit yourself,' Derek replied without offence. 'I think your Mum's in that end door. See you later maybe.' Carly nodded. Derek seemed really nice and when he smiled, she felt the same warmth and affection she did with her mother. He continued

17

bouncing his ball as she wandered along the corridor to the door he'd indicated.

'Too tight, Joseph. I'll burst those stitches halfway down the walk,' Susan Morris's laugh echoed from behind the door which Carly stood outside. Hesitantly, she pushed it open to find her mother amid the glamorous clutter of models who were being dressed, prodded and resewn into the Designer's creations. The child stood momentarily speechless, drinking in the sight of bustle and confusion which the cool ease of the parade concealed.

Back in the auditorium, Samantha sensed her twin had reached her destination.

'When's Carly coming back Daddy?' she innocently asked her father.

'Coming back?' George echoed. 'What do you mean ... coming back? Where is she?' he queried in disbelief, finally noticing the empty chair next to Samantha's.

'I think she said something about seeing Mum,' Samantha demurely stammered out, sounding just hesitant enough to keep up the concerned sister act.

'That little trouble maker,' George mumbled

angrily, grabbing a smirking Samantha by the hand and trying to slip quietly from the hall.

'I told her not to go Daddy. But she just wouldn't listen,' Samantha added with a glint of victory in her eye.

Unaware of her father's impending arrival, Carly's face broke into a broad smile as her mother saw her at the dressing room door and invited her in.

'Darling, this is what I do when I've been away from you all those unbearably long weeks at a time,' Susan said as she bent to kiss and hug her daughter.

'Oh mummy, you look . . . like a princess from a fairytale,' Carly whispered as she placed her small hand on her mother's radiant face. Susan laughed.

'It's just a trick . . . like magic . . .' she assured her daughter. 'You're the one who is a princess, sweetheart.' And then as Carly stood in awe, her mother called proudly to the rest of the dressing room: 'Look everyone, this is my beautiful daughter Carly!' Everyone waved or called 'hello' through the bustle of dressing and pinning, and all the while, Susan stood gazing admiringly at Carly.

'She's certainly a heart-breaker, Susie,' said the man who had been stitching Susan's dress.

'Thanks Joseph, I think so,' Susan replied as she placed a protective arm around Carly's shoulder. Carly couldn't believe all this was happening. Her mother was so loving and when she was with her, she felt so good. But at the sight of her father's figure, seething with anger as he stood at the open door of the dressing room, her happiness suddenly evaporated.

'Daddy,' she gasped, as if caught out with her hand in the cookie jar.

'George, Carly came to visit and . . .' Susan was cut off mid sentence as George lunged for Carly, grabbing her by the arm.

'You will never learn will you?' he shouted at his daughter.

'No, Daddy please let me stay with mummy,' Carly pleaded.

'Let her go George,' Susan commanded, taking George by surprise. His grip slackened slightly and Carly wriggled away, running through the room and upturning a couple of make-up cases in the process.

'That damned brat of yours,' George spat at Susan as he took chase.

'Don't worry Mum,' Samantha meekly whispered to the distressed figure of her mother. 'I'm here.'

They both watched as first Carly, and then George, disappeared through the door at the end of the room. Samantha clung to her mother, comforting her. She was elated by the success of her plan. Carly couldn't have been more of a stupid idiot if she'd tried.

Carly could hear her father's footsteps echoing on the tiled floor somewhere behind her. It was dark in this passageway and she had no idea to where she was running anyway. In her anxiety, she fell through the curtains before her and found herself on the catwalk in a tangle of organza and chiffon, the outfits being displayed by three of the models currently parading. The child's shrieks of fear and embarrassment were initially amusing to the audience and an odd camera flash exploded as her small figure hesitantly tried to make its way long the long raised platform.

'Carly!' screamed a voice from behind her. Her father had even pursued her on to the

catwalk. This knowledge propelled her for-
wards and she began to quicken her pace.
She ran between two of the surprised models,
knocking over a large pot plant which in
turn overbalanced a Grecian statuette. The
audience were no longer amused, as debris
began flying in all directions. Pandemonium
broke loose in the hall as people rose from
their seats to avoid being hit by breaking
scenery. As George reached Carly, he
grabbed her from behind, lifting her by the
shoulders. The trapped child was shocked by
his grip and screamed, kicked and punched
at her father, her fear suddenly overcome by
her instincts of self preservation – she had
felt his physical wrath on other occasions.
And all the while, the cameras snapped and
flashed recording Carly's removal from the
stage, frame by frame.

'What a field day the Press will have with
the spectacle you provided,' George yelled
disgustedly at Carly as he threw her into the
back of the car outside the auditorium. 'You
little horror, don't think you'll get away
with this! You just wait 'till I get you home!'
But the child was sobbing so violently that
she heard nothing of her father's threats.

In bed that night. Carly lay trance-like, listening to her parents fight in the distance in their bedroom. She had been saved from her father's pledged physical thrashing by her mother's intervention. Her father had stood with a leather belt in his hand and rage in his eyes, held at bay by his wife, whose words rose in defence of Carly. And all the while, Samantha had stood beside her father, mute. She seemed almost expectant, a glint in her eye betraying her pleasure at her sister's imminent punishment. Carly noticed this. She had often wondered about Samantha, who seemed only to be truly happy when Carly was in hot water. She stood looking into her sister's face, trying to understand this. As her parents threw abuse, 'it' was said. George launched the missile at Susan, but it hit and exploded upon Carly as surely as if she were its target.

'I never wanted your second brat,' he'd said. 'Samantha should have been an only child.' And then Carly saw the smile of superiority break all over Samantha's face until, in hurt confusion and rejection, Carly had looked away.

Her father's words re-echoed in Carly's head now as she lay in the room she shared with her twin. '. . . I never wanted your second brat ... Samantha should have been an only child ... an only child.' And as the din from the fighting of their parents again rose, Carly turned in bed to look across at the favoured Samantha. But it was no longer the face of her sister she saw, but the face of her enemy. Samantha was lying quite still, eyes wide open as she listened to every word of her parents' fight, wearing a smile of cunning and delight.

chapter two

The years which followed Carly's first knowledge of her father's rejection ground by
slowly for her. Carly watched as her sister
Samantha mesmerized everyone she met.
Samantha basked in the favoured attentions
of her father. And whenever Carly resisted
her sister's plans or wants, Samantha
needled Carly with the 'I should have been
an only child' line. That always stung, and
usually Carly's efforts to stand up for herself
simply evaporated. Carly drew more and
more into her shell. Only with her mother
and her friend, Derek, could she ever feel
really happy. It was funny about Derek, he
had popped up in her life at the most un-
expected moments. Sometimes, he would
arrive at the house accompanying his father
who had been signed under contract by the
Morris Agency. 'Well, if nothing else . . . at
least your father can spot talent,' Derek had
once quipped to Carly with a laugh.

And when Carly had been taken by her mother to functions which the fashion houses had put on to launch a new line or product, suddenly there would be Derek, trailing after his father who was also a guest. Carly had always thought of Derek as a friend, a confidant. She'd poured out her heart to him over the years, revealing the painful truth of her family relationship with her father and Samantha. But lately Carly had noticed something more in her feelings for Derek. He was fourteen now and she was only six months younger. Suddenly they didn't want to push and prod each other in a rough and tomboy way anymore. Now they secretly held hands and hugged each other when no one was around. Samantha had walked in on them once and Carly saw something in her sister's eyes that clearly indicated her jealousy.

Samantha, with all her confidence and outgoing personality, had a throng of boys chasing her. But suddenly, she had noticed Derek. Mostly, she was attracted by the fact that it was Carly he favoured. And this was something Samantha intended to set right. At first, she was subtle, trying to provoke Derek's interest in her, parading before the boy each time he was nearby. Behind her back Carly and Derek had laughed at Samantha's devious ways, feeling safe and confident in their own growing friendship. But then Samantha literally threw herself at the boy. Carly knew Derek had no interest in her sister, but Samantha's crusade was beginning to unnerve her. Why couldn't Samantha be happy with what she already had in her life and leave Carly a little happiness of her own? But the scheming girl continued to make life miserable for Carly. Finally Carly's distress spilled over and she felt Derek was too close to the situation to understand her mounting worries. In desperation, she decided to seek her mother's advice. 'Yes sweetheart, I've noticed your sister's little campaign to win Derek over,' Susan assured Carly. 'But I think you're handling it just fine. She can't win. You know that. That boy is your friend, not hers!' Somehow it was good to hear someone else say it. Fortunately her mother knew just what Samantha was about. Samantha's relationship with her father had thrown her parents' marriage out of balance. More and more often, hostility arose between George and Susan. Usually, the two were barely speaking except for the sake of public appearances. And however their quarrels began, inevitably they would include the subject of the twins. George would hurl abuse at Susan, regarding what he saw as her over-protection of Carly. But Susan's views on his favouritism of Samantha would fall on deaf ears. Day in, day out, the Morris house was becoming more a battle ground than a home. And so Susan and Carly had drawn closer together, sensing their like positions as opponents of a similar foe. They enjoyed their moments together as mother and daughter. Somehow the world of hostility in which they were both forced to live was overcome by the tenderness they shared. This perhaps was the seed of Samantha's continuing resentment of Carly. No matter what she had done in life, Samantha had failed to win her mother's favours. Her mother had always seemed to know just what was happening, and helped that weakling Carly out of every mess that Samantha had helped her into. Samantha was pondering this fact as she lay in the darkness of her room she still shared with Carly, listening to her sister sleep. She often listened to Carly through the night, hearing the whimpering cry of fear sometimes rise from her in sleep. That was the only part of sharing a room with her twin that Samantha enjoyed. She'd begged her father to give her a room of her own, but he'd insisted that she stay with Carly just to keep her eye on things. And she'd managed to keep Carly under her thumb pretty well all through the years. There were only two obstacles to Samantha's complete control of Carly: their mother and Derek Peterson. But her plans for Derek were well under way. Perhaps later she could turn her attentions back to winning over her mother. But Derek must come first. The dance coming up at Bermington Ladies College would be just the occasion to make her move. Samantha was sure she could outshine her sister. Derek would forget all this kid-stuff romance he thought he had for Carly, when he could see how much more mature Samantha was. She could stun everyone, of that she was sure. She'd have Derek Peterson eating out of her hand in no time. And he'd finally recognize Carly for the wimp she really was. Carly stirred in bed, suddenly breaking Samantha's train of thought. And as she looked across at her sleeping sister, Samantha thought she could see the smile of contentment play across Carly's face.

'Dream on, sister,' she whispered aloud. 'Soon all you'll have left will be nightmares.' And then Samantha too drifted off to sleep.

Carly awoke the following morning to find

Samantha's bed already empty. It was a relief. Her sister's absence made life a far more pleasant prospect. She stretched lazily, thinking of Derek. But a light tapping on her bedroom door distracted her. 'Come in,' she called drowsily.

'I hoped you'd be awake,' her mother whispered as she closed the door behind her. 'I heard Samantha leave early this morning with your father and I wanted to give you something without an audience.'

Carly watched as Susan produced a large silver striped box from behind her back.

'Oh mum, what is it?'

'Open it and find out!' Susan said excitedly, as she pulled open the curtains allowing the glow of early morning sunlight to fill the room. Susan watched as her daughter patiently untied the strings and opened the lid to reveal the electric blue silk and taffeta dress she had so carefully chosen the day before.

'Oh, mum it's beautiful ... I've never seen such a wonderful dress − I love it ... thank you! thank you!' Carly shrieked with pleasure as she flung her arms about her mother and kissed her.

'Well, with the Ladies College formal being your first dance Carly, I just wanted you to look and feel as special as you are,' Susan smiled at her daughter.

'But what about Sam?' Carly asked, as a shadow moved across the morning sun.

'Don't you worry, Samantha can fend for herself,' Susan assured her. Susan's motherly instincts had alerted her to Samantha's current plans, and she knew Carly would be an easy mark. George had nurtured a sophistication in Samantha which was missing in her twin sister. Susan knew just how important Derek was to Carly. They were close and Samantha was trying to split them up. This dress was just an insurance against that happening.

'Can we keep this dress as our secret for now, mum?' Carly asked quietly. 'I want Sam's eyes to pop when she sees it on the night.'

'I think that's a great idea and it won't only be Samantha's eyes that will pop out. Just wait till Derek sees you in this!' Susan laughed as Carly smiled broadly, feeling things were about to swing her way for a change.

*

Two days before the night of the dance, Samantha was wandering the empty house listlessly. Carly was off with their mother somewhere and her father was at a meeting. Even the housekeeper had been called away. It was raining outside and Samantha felt just as dismal an atmosphere indoors. She had finally decided to go to the formal with Collin Jensen. She'd been asked by four different boys, but just today she'd decided Collin was dumb enough to fit well into her plans for Derek and Carly. But something just wasn't right! Samantha had sensed a growing and unusual confidence in Carly. Her sister had spent a lot of time with their mother over the past week and Samantha's instincts told her something was up. But what? She couldn't figure it out. None of her old tricks annoyed Carly any more. Even when she'd picked up the extension on Carly's call with Derek, Carly just laughed and said they had finished talking anyway. Yes, something was most definitely going on, Samantha was sure of that.

She decided to console herself by trying on the necklace her father had bought her to wear to the dance. It was an 18 ct gold antique chain set with three heart shaped diamonds. Just wait till Carly laid her eyes on this necklace, Samantha thought with a smirk as she admired herself in the dressing room mirror. And with the white crepe dress she'd picked out, she'd set everyone off their feet. Poor pathetic Carly. Samantha almost felt a twinge of sisterly sympathy, imagining what Carly would look like standing next to her. She flung open her sister's wardrobe, skimming through clothes she felt were too immature for herself, wondering what on earth Carly would wear to the dance. Then she spotted the silver striped box bearing the fashion-house name, Camouflaged in the back of the cupboard. She hastily grabbed it and threw its contents on the dressing-room couch. The electric blue dress spilled out in all its silken taffeta beauty. 'That slimy snake!' Samantha spat out the words, her heart beating with frustration and anger. She held up the dress taking in its full magnificence. Suddenly she realized the possibility that Carly might outshine her. 'Well if she thinks she's going to wear this, she can think again!' Samantha hissed aloud as she clutched a pair of scissors from the table, ready to shred the creation before her. But suddenly she stopped, silently plotting an alternative ... a better revenge. A smile of cunning spread across her face as she folded the dress and replaced it carefully in its box, noting the name and address of the store on the lid. The rain outside was clearing as she left the house and Samantha was glad to see the sun breaking through.

The night of the dance finally arrived. Susan Morris waited impatiently in the loungeroom for her daughters. Both had insisted upon dressing for the dance alone. Carly had taken over her mother's dressing room, while Samantha had used the one attached to the bedroom she shared with Carly.

As Carly walked into the room, Susan stood up and gasped with pride: 'Oh . . . Carly, you look wonderful . . . I've never seen anyone so beautiful.' Susan's eyes began to fill with tears of happiness, as Carly smiled and twirled around in a circle of pure joy before her mother, becoming an electric blue flash of loveliness through Susan's blurred vision.

But the euphoria of the moment instantly dissolved as Samantha entered the room. Both Susan and Carly stood momentarily mute; disbelief written upon their faces. Samantha wore exactly the same dress as Carly. Susan and Carly remained suspended in shock as Samantha coolly fingered her gold and diamond necklace, making sure her audience noticed the extra trimming which she felt set her outfit above that of her twin.

'Samantha! How could you?' Susan angrily asked her daughter breaking the silence. 'You've copied your sister's dress just to upset her!'

'I don't know what you mean, mother. I bought this dress weeks ago for the dance tonight,' Samantha innocently replied, pretending her own amazement. Just then, George Morris stuck his head around the door. 'What's up?' he said, more to his favourite daughter than to anyone else in the room.

'Well look daddy, Carly's wearing my dress!' Samantha quickly said, feigning distress.

'Your little pet has gone too far this time,' Susan shouted at her husband. 'She's bought the same dress as Carly ... and where did she get that jewellery?' she added with a glare.

'I bought it for her just as you buy things for your Carly, Susan,' George replied defensively. 'And as for the dresses – well, I guess it's just coincidence. Carly will just have to change. That's all!'

'I'm not changing,' Carly shrieked.

'And neither am I!' Samantha echoed jubilantly, thinking of how her necklace set off the dress which really looked much plainer on Carly. The refusal of each twin to change further fuelled the glaring and insults which raged between their parents. And as the College car arrived to pick up the twins, they drove off in their identical dresses, leaving their parents consumed in a blazing argument.

Not a word passed between the girls on their journey to the dance. Carly wore a look of determination matched by Samantha's smirk of superiority. On arrival, they entered the College hall and attracted the attention of everyone they passed. As they stood waiting for their escorts at the top of the main staircase into the ballroom, they kept up a wall of silence. Carly saw Derek making his way towards her and she prayed he wouldn't make a big thing of the dresses.

'Hi, Carly,' Derek waved as he approached.

'Hi,' Carly smiled, as she felt his eyes drinking in her image approvingly.

'You look wonderful, Carly. You must be the

most beautiful girl here. Gosh I can't believe I could be so lucky!' Derek exclaimed, as he smiled directly into Carly's eyes. 'And if Samantha can wait by herself, I think we'd better dance,' he added. It was as though he hadn't even seen Samantha at all. He hadn't seen anyone else – only Carly. Samantha was livid. Anger rose up within her as she watched the 'happy couple' make their way down the staircase like Cinderella and her Handsome Prince. She had to grit her teeth to smother her need to yell abuse. But she'd get Carly yet! Only now it would be much worse. Her sister would regret ever coming to this dance, she'd see to that.

Samantha lumbered around the dance floor most of the night with that dummy Collin Jensen who, she'd discovered too late, had two left feet. But she'd needed to maintain a surveillance of her sister and Derek, awaiting her opportunity to spring her trap. The pair had danced all night long looking only at each other. Samantha nearly gave up a couple of times, especially as the oaf Collin, had already bruised her feet so badly that she had been forced to hobble. But finally, with relief, she saw Carly make her way towards the ladies' powder room while Derek headed for the punch bowl.

'I've got to go to the loo,' she said, hastily pushing the clammy Collin away from her and following her sister from the room.

Fortunately, Monica Sutcliffe was sitting in the outer lounge of the ladies, applying lipstick, when Samantha entered. Monica was one of Samantha's friends from the College and she knew her help would be easy to obtain. 'Hi Monica,' Samantha whispered. 'Have you seen my sister, Carly?'

'Sure, she's in the loo,' Monica replied, her voice lowered sensing that something was up. Monica loved practical jokes so when Samantha explained the one she had planned for Carly, the naïve girl was eager to help.

When Carly came back into the powder room she found both Samantha and Monica waiting for her and, before she knew what had happened, they had locked her into a side cupboard. She screamed and thumped on the door for a while but it was useless. And then Monica's voice announced: 'It's just for half an hour Carly, so keep calm.'

Samantha slipped the necklace from around her neck and put it in her handbag. She looked into the mirror and rearranged her hair slightly and wiped off the lipstick which Carly never wore.

'That should do it,' She said to her reflection, as Monica gave her a laugh of approval.

She returned to the ballroom and searched the crowd for Derek, passing the oaf Collin without a glance.

'Hi, what took you so long, I missed you,' Derek whispered as she reached him.

'Sorry, there was a queue out there,' she said apologetically, mimicking her sister's actions by placing her arm around Derek's waist. Samantha smiled inwardly to herself, thinking just how easy it was to impersonate such a wimp as Carly. Derek led her back to the dance floor, unaware of the fact that she wasn't Carly. He sang along with a couple of the songs as they danced, hugging her during the slow numbers.

'Gosh it's hot in here,' Samantha said in Carly's manner of talking. 'Do you think we could get some fresh air, Derek?'

'Sure, Carly. Come on, we'll go out to the verandah,' Derek agreed as he took her by the hand and led her through the crowd.

*

The moon was full as they walked out into the coolness of the night. Samantha put her arms around Derek's neck. 'Gosh, this isn't like you, Carly,' he stammered in surprise.

'Well maybe I've grown up tonight,' she said as she began to kiss him on the ear and cheek. 'I think we're ready for more than hugs and holding hands?' she added before she kissed him on the lips. The boy responded gently and then hugged her to him. 'Oh Carly you're so beautiful and such a lovely person as well, I can't believe how lucky I am to have you.' But Samantha wanted more.

'Well, kiss me properly then,' she murmured as she pressed her lips upon his more passionately. And over Derek's shoulder, Samantha spotted the dishevelled figure of her sister, who had been released from the cupboard right on cue.

Carly stood, watching from the dim shadows as Derek kissed Samantha over and over. She was paralysed by the shock of such a sight. She felt betrayed, flattened. How could Derek do this after everything she'd told him? It was like a nightmare, not real. Maybe she would wake up in a second and this image would dissolve. But then she felt Samantha's eyes upon her and she looked back at her sister whose arms were around Derek. Over Derek's shoulder, Samantha continued to glare at Carly triumphantly until Carly could stand it no more. She ran through the doors, up the stairs and out into the cover of the night. And only Samantha heard Derek murmur: 'Oh Carly, you'll always be the only girl for me.'

Over the next week, Carly retreated into her shell even more. She refused to take any of Derek's calls and walked around the house like a zombie. Susan noticed her daughter's distress but although she tried, she failed to extract any information from either Carly or Samantha on the subject. When Carly approached her mother asking about being sent to a boarding school, Susan was at first shocked. But as the nightly fights between herself and George continued, she began to give Carly's request more serious consideration. If she allowed Carly to leave, it might give the child a chance to get out of this incessant hostility. Finally she decided to agree. In between his ranting and raving, she mentioned it to George, who'd jumped at the chance to get rid of 'the unwanted brat'. Susan was again stabbed in the heart by his callousness but if it achieved some good for Carly, it didn't matter how or why it came about.

About two weeks after the night of the dance, the phone rang again. Samantha and Carly were alone at home. Carly was packing for boarding school.

'It's Derek again,' Samantha announced to Carly's back.

'I'm not in,' Carly replied without turning. She couldn't bear to look at Samantha now.

'OK!' Samantha said coolly, as she went back to the phone. Then an idea hit her. 'Hello,' she said quietly into the receiver.

'Carly?' Derek's voice asked.

'Yes,' Samantha replied in a distressed way.

'I'm sorry Carly ... it was a trick, honest! She pretended to be you,' Derek blurted out on the end of the phone. Samantha smothered her own amusement and then continued her act as Carly, saying in a sombre voice: 'Well, Derek if you can't tell the difference between us after all this time, I don't want to know you anyway. I never want to see you again! Goodbye Derek.'

'But Carly ...' Derek's voice stammered as

Samantha hung up the 'phone quietly. That should do it, she decided. Tomorrow Carly would be gone and that would be that!

Samantha walked out on to the driveway with her mother and father to wave goodbye to Carly the following morning. She had always maintained the loving sister act just for appearances. Carly embraced her mother and formally farewelled her father before she left. She didn't look at Samantha. And as the car drove out of sight, Samantha continued to wave all the while as she asked her father: 'Daddy, why does Carly hate me so? I've never done anything to deserve it!'

George Morris looked down at his favourite daughter and shrugged. 'Your sister has problems, darling. Maybe we'll all be better off without her.' Samantha hugged her father with a smile of triumph upon her face. And as George glanced over at his wife, her narrowed gaze conveyed her repulsion of them both. Susan Morris walked inside and slammed the door.

chapter three

Susan Morris drove herself to the boarding school. Driving had become an escape for her. As she watched the kilometres mount on her speedo, measuring her distance from home, she began to relax. During the six months since Carly had left for boarding school, Susan's situation at home had worsened. Samantha had become more forceful, enjoying her 'only child' status in the family to the hilt. The precocious teenager now joined in the quarrels which erupted between her parents, always supporting her father's condemnation of her mother. To Susan, it seemed that since Carly had 'escaped', both Samantha and George had turned their venom solely upon her. But Susan was determined that Carly should remain unaware of this fact. She didn't want her daughter to feel obliged to return home just for her sake. Judging from her letters, Carly was much better off right where she was. The early letters spelt out Carly's bitterness, and at first Susan thought she might have made a mistake in sending Carly away. But gradually the mood of Carly's writing had changed. And during the months that followed, the girl had obviously risen above the oppressive influence of her home to find a happiness and confidence Susan had never thought possible for her shy daughter. As she swung the car through the heavy iron gates of Carly's school, Susan steeled herself to maintain her composure. Carly must be assured that all was well at home; Susan loved her too much to ever want her to come back to that house.

'Yes Mrs Morris, I can assure you that your daughter is a real favourite among the staff here,' the Headmistress said to Susan some time later. 'And she's such a kind and tolerant girl. I imagine you're very proud of her.'

'I certainly am,' Susan agreed enthusiastically, as she walked outside with Mrs Holt. 'And I can't tell you how pleased I am that she's settled in so well here. Thank you, Mrs Holt, I'll see you again on my next visit,' she added as she shook hands politely and walked to rejoin a beaming Carly. The girl was surrounded by a group of friends but she broke away and ran to meet her mother.

'Oh mum, isn't she nice?' Carly chuckled as she hugged her mother.

Susan couldn't believe the change in Carly. She'd noticed it as soon as she'd arrived and Carly had ran laughing into her arms. The sullenness had gone. Her daughter was truly happy, Susan thought with pleasure. And as Carly introduced her mother to all the girls, she was so confident and assured, it made Susan forget all the troubles of home.

Mother and daughter stayed together that night in town and only once did Carly look a little sad when she asked her mother if she'd ever seen Derek.

'He called after you'd left and I told him where you'd gone ... but that was all,' Susan said. Carly had looked a little crestfallen for a moment, but then she bounced back. And it was Susan who was upset as she dropped Carly back to the school the following morning. She stroked her daughter's hair, wishing she never had to leave her. The girl was growing so fast, she didn't want to miss a day of being with her.

*

Carly sensed her mother's distress. 'Oh . . . mum, don't worry, it's only two months till the long Christmas break. I'll be home with you for six weeks then. OK?' Carly whispered to her mother while she hugged her.

'OK sweetheart, see you then,' Susan called as she drove off reluctantly. But in the back of her mind, she wondered how she could save Carly from ever having to return home again.

Carly wrote often during the next two months, explaining the various tests she was undertaking and giving her mother snippets of information about her friends. And right on schedule, she arrived home two weeks before Christmas to find the house as hostile as ever and her mother looking ill.

'How long have you been sick, Mum?' Carly asked as she joined Susan in her sitting room for a private chat.

'Oh, I'm not really sick darling, just tired, I've been working non-stop since I saw you in October.' Susan assured Carly, just as George broke into the room suddenly, surprised to find Carly at home at all.

'You never mentioned she was coming home, Susan,' he accused his wife, pointing dramatically at Carly.

'Dad, it's Christmas,' Carly said, trying to maintain a semblance of peace.

'OK. Well, stick to your part of the house, eh?' George commanded gruffly.

'Alright, I will!' Carly replied as pleasantly as she could.

'Now off with you, your mother has to rest. She's due back at the studio at three o'clock,' George said as he tried to push Carly out of the room. But the girl turned on him defiantly.

'She can't work today, Dad. She's sick. Anyone can see that!' Carly hissed at her father angrily.

'We're in the middle of a major campaign, Carly. Your mother hasn't the time to be sick!' George announced, both for the benefit of his daughter and his wife.

'George, I really don't think I can get there today,' Susan interrupted, looking more pale by the moment. Her husband surveyed her face and noticed it was drained of colour.

'Look I'll get a Doctor to come by and give you something! That should keep you happy!' George said to his wife with an edge of sarcasm, as he ushered Carly out of the room and shut the door.

Carly hastily unpacked her clothes and awaited the arrival of the Doctor. But Samantha kept pestering her, letting her own feelings about their mother's illness be known.

'She's only trying to get attention. Dad and I know all her tricks. She's weak and that's where you inherited your weakness from!' Samantha said to her sister haughtily.

'Shut up! Just shut up Samantha!' Carly screamed as the door bell finally rang.

Carly anxiously showed the Doctor to her mother's room. But her father stepped in and closed the door on her again.

Five minutes later, the Doctor left. And as George showed him out, Carly slipped back to her mother. 'Just a vitamin deficiency, he said, Carly,' her mother consoled the worried child. 'He gave me some multi-vitamin shots and said I'm to take one of these pills if I start to feel tired.'

Carly picked up the bottle of tablets by her mother's bedside. 'Mum, these are "uppers". I've seen them before. A couple of kids at school have had them,' Carly screeched anxiously. 'You're not taking these!' she added, heading towards the bathroom.

*

George re-entered the room just as Carly flushed the contents of the bottle down the toilet. He looked at the empty bottle in Carly's hand.

'What the hell? . . . Where are your mother's pills, Carly?' George stammered in disbelief.

'She's not taking uppers!' Carly yelled at her father, as she saw a guilty look cross his face. 'You knew, didn't you!' she hissed at him. 'You knew they were uppers! I suppose you paid that Doctor extra to give them to her,' Carly accused, throwing the empty bottle on to the floor.

'How dare you! You little brat! That school certainly hasn't helped you to change,' George yelled as he moved towards his daughter.

'And all you care about is Mum finishing that shoot . . . You couldn't give a damn about whether or not she's sick . . . You don't care about anyone but yourself and your precious agency!' Carly continued. George was now directly in front of her and, as Carly looked into his face, she saw the madness of rage in his eyes. She didn't see him raise his hand. But suddenly she felt the slap across her face which sent her sprawling to the floor.

'No!' Susan screamed from the bed as she looked at the crumpled heap upon the floor which was Carly. The girl was momentarily stunned. Her father had never before struck her.

'Don't you touch her again!' Susan warned, as she shakily clambered towards her daughter. But Carly regained her composure, rose to her feet, and stood before her father defiantly.

'If ever you do that to me again,' she shrieked at him with hatred in her eyes, 'I'll hit you back!' And then she calmly pushed past her father, walked out of the room and closed the door.

Carly's cool exterior soon dissolved as she reached the sanctuary of her own room. She was grateful for Samantha's absence as she laid on her bed and sobbed into her pillow for what seemed like hours. It was sheer torture in this house. If it wasn't for her mother, she'd never come back again. But her mother needed her. Those 'uppers' were proof of that. If she'd not been around, heaven knows what could have happened. Her father was capable of almost anything: she'd realized that now. She rubbed her face gently. She could still feel the imprint of her father's hand which had burnt into her skin as surely as if she'd been branded with his mark. Her hatred of him rose up within her again, threatening to erupt like a volcano.

She'd have to get out of here. Just for a while. Cindy Grey, a girl from boarding school, had asked Carly to phone her over the holidays. Now seemed just the time to arrange a meeting. Maybe they could go to that new up-market place in Jamison Court, 'Alibaba's'. It catered for an exclusive clientele: burgers and fries were served on silverware. Carly lifted the receiver and started dialling Cindy's number, unaware that Samantha had been listening and watching from their dressing room the whole time.

'It has been so easy,' Samantha thought to herself as she hastily dressed. Just after Carly had left, she'd called Derek and apologized for her inexcusable behaviour all those months ago at the dance. He was such a sap. He'd taken the bait: hook, line and sinker. Even though he'd hesitated when she'd suggested they meet so she could apologize in person, the lure of news about Carly had snagged him well and truly. That poor sap obviously still thought he could get Carly back. Well, today should put an end to that dream, and rub salt into Carly's wounds as well. Samantha smiled at herself in the mirror. It had been a brainwave to arrange to meet Derek outside 'Alibaba's', the place where she'd heard Carly arranging to meet some girl called Cindy. That way when she walked in with Derek, Carly couldn't help but notice them. And Carly would put two and two together ... and bingo! Samantha visualized Carly again rushing off in a flood of tears. But she glanced at her watch. She'd have to hurry; it wouldn't do for Derek to arrive before her.

Inside 'Alibaba's', Carly talked to Cindy, relaxing in the company of the bright, witty girl. She began to smile and laugh, just as she did at school. And this place was really radical, although you practically needed your own credit cards to pay for the fast food they served here.

'Gosh, Carly, that must be your twin sister,' Cindy suddenly said, pointing towards the figures that had just entered the front door. 'Just like her. She probably followed me down ...' Carly broke off in mid-sentence as she turned to see Samantha walking into the restaurant with Derek Peterson.

'Wow! Who's the guy she's with, Carls? He's

a real spunk!' Cindy whispered. But Carly rose from her seat and mumbled to Cindy that she was sorry but she'd have to leave. The old hurt was still there, and Carly fought back the tears as she began to make her way towards the front door. To her, it was just like the dance all over again. But in her haste, she caught her jacket on an empty chair which clattered noisily to the marble floor as she endeavoured to free herself from its grasp. It was then that Derek glanced over and spotted her. He was up and at the door before she could escape.

'Carly, I didn't see you. How are you?' he stammered.

'Obviously you didn't see me, Derek,' she snapped back at the boy. 'But then I guess Samantha looks the same anyway,' she added sarcastically as she tried to push past. But Derek grabbed Carly by the arm.

'Please, Carly, I really need to talk to you,' he begged her. Carly looked for a moment into Derek's pleading eyes. Then something clicked in her head and she again saw him on the verandah at the dance, kissing Samantha. A waiter passed them, carrying a tray of mega shakes and burgers. Instinctively, Carly grabbed a shake from the tray and upturned it on Derek's head. He released his hold on her in surprise. She didn't look back as she ran through the doors. It was already dark and she simply wanted to vanish into the night.

Derek was still dripping with milk shake as he reached the doors of 'Alibaba's and saw Carly turn towards the park across the street. He attempted to push his way through the doors to follow her as Samantha's arm reached out to stop him.

'Haven't you done enough, Samantha!' Derek exclaimed to the girl who, although she resembled Carly physically, was really nothing like her at all.

'I don't know what you mean, Derek. But look at yourself, you simply can't walk around dripping with chocolate milk,' Samantha explained with a laugh, as she played for time. If Derek was to catch Carly now, it could ruin everything. He might learn the truth and then they'd be back to square one, with Derek and Carly an item again. And Samantha couldn't tolerate that!

But although she fluttered her eyelashes at him, and attempted to wipe off some of the shake from his face, Derek threw Samantha off and pushed past her, disappearing into the night.

'Damn them!' Samantha cursed under her breath, as the waiter asked her to return and pay for the food and damages incurred by her friends.

By the time Derek found Carly in the park, she was no longer in a temper. At first she tried to escape him but he insisted she stay and at least give him a hearing. He watched her face as he spoke, telling her of Samantha's trick and the way she had impersonated her sister.

'Honest, Carly, I really thought she was you. I would never have kissed . . .' Derek said as his voice broke off huskily. Carly looked at the boy before her. She'd known him almost her whole life. He was a wonderful, caring person. Then she thought of Samantha – a devious, hostile, self-centred demon.

'And then when you said what you did on the phone,' Derek began. But Carly interrupted: 'Said what on the phone?' she asked in surprise.

'That you never wanted to see me again,' Derek replied. 'Well you sounded so definite, and I . . .'

'But Derek, I haven't spoken to you since that night at the dance,' Carly said in amazement. Then a light went on in Derek's head. 'It was her, again!' Derek exclaimed, as he paced angrily. 'God, she's as low as they come!'

'Don't I know it!' Carly agreed. 'Still, she didn't succeed, did she?' she added as she looked up at Derek and took his hand.

'Oh, Carly,' Derek murmured as he drew her to him and they hugged. 'Thank heaven, you're back!'

'Yes, I'm back!' Carly echoed Derek's words, suddenly elated. She was with Derek again and that was all that mattered for the moment.

'But I think we should have it out with Samantha right now!' Derek said angrily.

'No, Derek,' she whispered calmly. 'I can settle things with my sister in my own way.'

Derek looked down at Carly. She'd changed. She was stronger than she used to be. The time away had released an independent side to her character. He smiled. But underneath, she was still his Carly. And that was what was blowing his brain at the moment: He and Carly were together again.

*

Carly climbed into bed that night and waited for Samantha's return. About eleven o'clock, she heard her sister coming along the hallway to their room. No doubt she'd been off somewhere, licking her wounds. Carly knew that if there was one thing that annoyed Samantha it was for one of her little plans to fail. As the bedroom door swung open, Carly decided to put her own plan into action.

'I suppose Derek found you!' Samantha snapped as she entered the room.

'Derek?' Carly queried with feigned bewilderment. 'Huh! If he had've come near me again, he'd have copped more than just a milk shake on his head!' Samantha stood with surprise written all over her face.

'So he didn't catch up with you?' Samantha asked with a wry smirk which Carly noticed.

'No,' Carly lied. 'And I never expect to see him again,' she added, as she turned her back on Samantha.

'Oh, I see,' Samantha said, clinically. 'Well, too bad. But then he's such a sap, anyway.'

Carly stiffened her jaw in an effort to keep her mouth shut. Now wasn't the time to say anything, no matter how much she wanted

to defend Derek and rip Samantha to shreds.
She pretended to sleep and waited.

Before long, Samantha was in bed, her
steady even breathing indicating that she
was soundly asleep. Quietly, Carly rose from
her bed, clasping in her hand the scissors
she had earlier hidden beneath her pillow.
She stood over her sleeping sister, hardly
daring to breathe. But she hesitated. Samantha looked so innocent when she was
asleep. All Carly had ever wanted was for
her sister to be her friend. Then she remembered all the terrible things Samantha
had done to her and steeled herself to continue. 'You deserve this, Samantha,' Carly
whispered. Then silently she began. And lock
by lock, strand by strand, she snipped away
Samantha's long blond hair. Finally only
jagged patches off stubble clung to her sleeping sister's head. Then Carly stood back,
satisfied with her work. 'That's for all the
agony you have caused others,' she whispered again, before she climbed back into
bed and returned to sleep.

Samantha woke suddenly. It was three-
thirty a.m. according to her bedside clock.
Her throat was dry and her mouth was
parched. She stumbled to the bathroom for

some water, squinting in the brightness of the fluorescent light. The water was icy and tasted so good. But as she returned the glass to the sink, she caught sight of herself in the mirror. She gasped with shocked horror. Who was that hag staring back at her from the mirror? Where was her hair? Her first scream was enough to wake the house. And within seconds, the twins and their parents were all face-to-face in the girls' bedroom.

Carly readily admitted her actions, explaining it was a matter of retaliation. She revealed Samantha's devious plans of manipulation: the way she'd messed up things between Derek and herself. But all George could see was his precious daughter's distress.

'How dare you do this to Samantha!' he shouted at Carly.

'And how dare she do what she did to Derek and me!' Carly shouted back.

But before another word could be spoken, George had hit Carly across the face. The girl reared back at her father so quickly, that he hardly realized she had struck him.

'George!' Susan screamed. 'That's enough now!'

But George's anger was unleashed. He grabbed Carly by the shoulders, throwing her on to the bed where he struck her over and over.

'George, please, 'Susan yelled, as she attempted to stop her husband.

But George turned on her too, striking her across the head and hurling her to the ground. When he looked back at his hated daughter, she was just a snivelling heap upon the bed. He was satisfied. He took a stunned Samantha by the hand and led her out to the hallway. He commanded his wife to follow and leave Carly to herself. Susan brushed her hand on Carly's head before she left. At least the physical violence had ceased and she didn't want to inflame George's anger again. He closed the door and locked Carly into the room. 'I'll see you in the morning, darling,' Susan called through the door, before George yelled at her to go to bed. He set up Samantha in the guest room before he too went back to bed.

Susan felt powerless. She couldn't even bear to look at her husband's figure as it climbed back into the bed they shared. How she loathed him. Perhaps if she waited till he was asleep, she could let Carly out. But then

what? As she grappled with her problem, a
nagging pain in Susan's side began to gather
force. At first she'd thought it was from her
fall when George had struck her. She'd
landed on her side and the pain had stabbed
instantly. But gradually, as the hours ticked
by, it worsened. By six o'clock, she could
stand it no longer and her moaning woke
George.

'What on earth!' George mumbled drowsily.
'For God's sake, Susan, haven't we had
enough drama for one night?'

'George, please, I need a doctor,' Susan
begged.

'It's just nerves. Now try and get back to
sleep, will you! I've got an important meeting
this morning,' he said, turning his back on
his wife.

But Susan continued to moan. 'I can't move,
please, I'm begging you, help me!'

'Susan, I know you, you'll do anything for
attention!' he answered gruffly. But when
he looked at his wife, and saw the lather of
perspiration on her, he decided to get her
some tea.

'A doctor, George, please!' she continued to
beg.

'You'll feel better after some tea. Now for Christ sake, just keep quiet, will you?' George snapped as he left the room and headed for the kitchen. But Susan's moaning continued. 'A doctor, please!' She called again, more loudly.

Carly heard her mother from her own prison cell. She began thumping on the door, yelling for her father to get her mother a doctor. Then suddenly the door was unlocked and flung open. She made to escape to her mother's bedroom but her father caught her and hit her again, telling her to shut-up if she didn't want further bruises.

And all the while, Susan continued to moan.

By eight o'clock, Susan's moaning had been replaced by screaming. George came back into the room to find his wife writhing in agony on the bed. He finally realized something was really wrong and called an ambulance.

Carly watched from the window as the ambulance drove out of the driveway. This was like a nightmare. She tried the phone. But her father had fixed that the night before. She was helpless. She thumped on the door, pleading with Samantha, whom she knew was still somewhere around the house. But it was no use. Hours passed as Carly's frustration grew.

Then she heard a car door and looked down from her window to see her father paying the taxi before it pulled away. Minutes later, the key turned in the door lock. She braced herself for another belting. But as the door opened and her father and Samantha entered the room, she knew it was worse than she'd even imagined.

'I must tell you both together,' George began, not looking at either of his daughters, 'that the ambulance was too late. Your mother had a ruptured appendix and died on the way to the hospital.' His voice was sombre and, perhaps to an outsider, he would have appeared genuinely grief-stricken. But Carly knew better! With a lump in her throat, she looked up into her father's eyes. He tried to look away but she held his gaze. 'My mother is dead?' Carly asked quietly, as she stared at her father with hatred. He nodded as she felt the tears begin to well within her. 'And you killed her!' she spat at him, accusingly. George flushed with guilt, shaking his head in denial. But Carly screamed at her father, more forcefully: 'You killed her! And I'm going to make sure everyone knows you did!' Then she fell on to the bed, sobbing, as Samantha and her father left the room.

chapter four

'Yes Mrs Holt that's right, I told the English class that my father had killed my mother,' Carly confirmed the facts with which the Headmistress had already been acquainted. Carly had been back at Boarding School for a fortnight and was determined to tell her story to anyone who would listen.

'But my dear, didn't the investigation into your mother's untimely and tragic death exonerate your father from any blame whatsoever?' Mrs Holt asked, more for Carly's benefit than for her own.

'My sister supported my father in his lies,' Carly explained, 'and then they passed me off as unbalanced, or crazy, or at least out of control . . . So that let them off the hook! But I know what really happened that night Mrs Holt and I won't rest till my mother's death has been paid for.'

'But you've been ill yourself, haven't you?'

the kindly Headmistress consoled Carly. She knew only too well how sick Carly had been from the report which Carly's father had forwarded in case the School should need it. 'Neurotic,' the Doctor had stated, 'with a deep resentment and hatred of both her father and sister.' Mrs Holt had read the report thoroughly, finding its contents almost incomprehensible, in light of the happy, and tolerant girl she had known as Carly Morris only last year. But then Carly returned and she saw how she had changed. Tragedy and grief had remoulded the child.

'I'm not sick, Mrs Holt,' Carly snapped defiantly as she rose from her chair. 'They kept saying that so that no one would believe me, don't you understand?'

'Of course I understand Carly. You lost your mother . . . we all understand how dreadful it must be for you. But life must continue now. You must put it all behind you.'

'No!' Carly yelled, hammering the desk with her fist. 'He killed her!'

'Calm down please, Carly,' Mrs Holt instructed. 'This behaviour of yours just can't continue.' Carly looked into the eyes of the elderly woman and saw wisdom. She sat down again.

'I'm sorry Mrs Holt,' she whispered.

'That's alright, my dear, but really now you'll have to behave more like a lady. You've been in trouble three times this week already. Bashing up the Perkins girl . . . and the incident with Mrs Glover in the Art room . . . and now this story you've read to your English class. Carly, I'm at my wits end.' Mrs Holt paused for a moment and looked at Carly. She had been such a wonderful student last year. When Mr Morris had rung and explained the situation with Carly, the Headmistress just couldn't believe her ears. To think that the child had actually attacked her own sister with a pair of scissors and cut off all her hair . . . and on the very night of her mother's death. But Carly's behaviour back at School had confirmed her violent tendency.

'Well, Carly,' Mrs Holt announced sympathetically, 'just one more chance then.'

'Yes, Mrs Holt,' Carly smiled, 'but I can't stop telling the truth,' she added.

'Carly, it is my advice to you to refrain from this slandering of your father. For, my child, ultimately, it will be you yourself who will suffer the consequences.'

Carly put her head down, feeling defeated. Of all the people here, she thought Mrs Holt would help. She remembered how much her mother had liked the old Headmistress.

'Now off with you, dear, or you'll miss dinner,' the Headmistress said kindly.

Carly rose and left the office without a word. What was the use? No one seemed to believe her. Only Derek was on her side but he couldn't prove anything either.

One by one, her friends at School tired of Carly. She was no longer any fun to be with. Only Cindy stuck by her.

'He did kill her, Cindy, as surely as he stuck a knife into her,' Carly said to her friend as they wandered past the hockey field one afternoon about a week later.

'If you say so, then I believe you,' Cindy assured her.

'Thanks,' Carly replied, 'I wish everyone was like you.'

'I wish everyone was like you,' echoed a voice from behind a tree. Suddenly a gang of year 10 girls appeared.

'Come off it, Morris. Why don't you lay off

this grieving daughter act. We've all had about as much as we can take,' said Janice Harper, the spokesperson of the group.

'My father killed my mother,' another girl mimmicked. Carly knew they were baiting her, but she couldn't help herself.

'Come on Carly,' Cindy called. But it was too late. Another heckle had been enough. Carly had lashed out at one of the girls and before she'd realized it, a teacher had appeared and dragged her off to the office again.

Her expulsion from the school was swift and almost painless. Mrs Holt explained her position to Carly. The Headmistress virtually had no choice.

By four o'clock the following afternoon, Carly again stood upon the doorstep of her own house, dreading the life that awaited her behind its doors. But she was fourteen years old and had nowhere else to go.

George confined Carly to the house. He employed a private tutor to instruct her during the day and locked her in her room at night. Samantha had moved into the guest room down the hall, so Carly's room was a prison of solitary confinement. That was the only part of the whole arrangement of which she approved.

Then the psychiatric counselling had begun. George had sought help from the same Police Psychiatrist who had assessed Carly after her mother's death. But Carly knew that this doctor believed in her father's innocence and her own neurotic tendency. He no longer even raised his eyebrows at her accusations regarding her father's responsibility for her mother's death. Finally he suggested medication.

'But I don't need any drugs, Dr Hume,' Carly had said in resistance.

'Carly, it's only for a short time,' the Doctor assured her condescendingly. At first the tablets had quietened Carly down, but gradually she began to cut out some of the doses without the doctor's knowledge. She flushed the extra pills down the toilet. And when her father carelessly forgot to lock her door one evening, presuming she had been drugged to sleep for the night, she slipped quietly downstairs and phoned the papers renewing her accusations about him to one of the reporters.

Unfortunately, George was phoned before

the story went to press. He explained his daughter's 'sorry' situation and killed the story.

'If you persist in this vendetta of yours,' he later threatened Carly, 'I will have no choice but to send you to a mental home.'

But Carly merely laughed at her father's pathetic threats.

'I mean it, Carly,' he continued. 'With Doctor Hume's recommendation and my signature, you could be in a State Hospital before you even realized what was happening. So lay off or you'll suffer the consequences.'

The door slammed on her again as her father left the room. But she wasn't going to be silenced so easily. After all, how much worse could things be in a mental ward? Her own home was a bad as a prison to her now.

She persisted in her accusations both to Dr Hume and to her tutor. Then she began writing out the events of that night on sheets of paper and throwing them from her window. Maybe the neighbours would be interested.

George found one of these sheets on his own

doorstep and two more blown by the breeze into the trees of his front garden.

In fury, he again lashed into Carly. 'You will submit,' he shouted at the girl as he beat her brutally with a leather belt.

'Never,' she cried as she raised her arms to protect her face. 'You killed my mother,' she sobbed as she fell again, a bruised and mangled heap upon her bed.

'I'm afraid Carly has taken to turning her rage upon herself,' George explained to the Police Psychiatrist when he arrived the following day. 'She lashed herself with a belt last night and she's given herself some pretty nasty bruises.'

Doctor Hume shook his head sadly. Well Mr Morris ,' he said softly after his examination of Carly, 'I really think it may be time to commit the girl. It's for her own safety now, I'm afraid.' George nodded his assent.

'I've given her an injection for now and I'll call by tomorrow,' Doctor Hume added as he left.

George closed the door and a smile of relief spread across his face. 'Finally! that brat could be locked away and he and Samantha could return to their normal lives.' He ran

upstairs to give Sam the good news. This
called for a celebration. With Carly under
sedation, perhaps he and Sam could slip out
to dinner somewhere and then before the
month was out, Carly would be out of their
lives forever.

Derek watched from a tree as George and
Samantha drove off in their Mercedes. He'd
tried for weeks to talk to Carly. But his
telephone calls were never returned and each
time he'd come to the house, he'd been turned
away by either Samantha or her father with
the excuse that Carly was out or in session
with her tutor or psychiatrist. Derek didn't
trust George Morris and so he'd decided to see
what was going on for himself. He waited till
the car was out of sight. Then he climbed
down and made his way around the side of
the house. He knew this house almost as well
as he knew his own. One of the windows
down this side was always left unlatched. He
had no trouble sliding inside, and wasted no
time in making his way to Carly's room. But
he found the door locked. There wasn't a
sound from inside. 'Carly,' he called softly as
he tapped on the door. Derek looked about the
dim hallway. And on the side table, below the
oval mirror, he found the key.

*

As he pushed open the door, Derek couldn't believe what he saw. Carly lay on her bed, a bruised and quivering wreck.

'Carly, Carly! wake up,' he whispered gently as he brushed the hair from the girl's face.

Carly's eyes opened but he could tell she'd been drugged.

'Derek,' she said in a strained voice. 'Oh, Derek, please save me!'

Derek helped Carly to the bathroom and bathed her face with cold water, trying to revive her to consciousness.

'Come on,' he finally whispered as he gathered her up in his arms. 'We're getting you out of here.'

Carly agreed drowsily as she hugged his neck. But just as they reached the top of the stairs, the front door opened. 'Shh,' Derek whispered as he ducked into an alcove still carrying Carly.

'I'll be OK Derek ... put me down ... we might have to run for it,' Carly suggested.

'Are you sure you'll be able to stand?' he whispered.

'Yes, that cold water did help,' she said as

she tottered a little but then regained her balance.

George had disappeared to the kitchen but Samantha was on her way up the stairs. 'I'll just be a minute, dad,' Samantha called as she passed by the alcove without noticing the concealed couple.

Silently Carly and Derek made their way down the stairs. They reached the front door safely, just as Samantha reached the top of the stairs and spotted them. 'Dad!' she screamed. But Derek was dragging Carly through the door.

'They're going to put me in a Mental Home, Derek,' Carly shouted, with fear on her face. 'We just have to escape, we can't fail.'

'We'll take the Merc,' Derek announced confidently.

'But can you drive?' Carly asked questioningly.

'Sure,' Derek assured her as they jumped in and he realized with relief that George Morris had left the keys in the ignition. Hot wiring wasn't in his repertoire. And as he was still only fourteen years old, neither was driving. But his dad often let him drive around up on the farm. He knew the moves.

*

Derek turned the engine over as Carly screamed that George was on his way.

The car seemed to rear up on its back wheels just before a stunned George Morris could reach them. 'Hurry Derek,' Carly shrieked as she watched the figures of her father and sister recede into the background.

'Where to?' he asked.

'Anywhere,' Carly said, 'as long as it's away from here.'

They drove north, keeping to the backroads as much as possible. But before long, they were forced onto the highway. Derek kept to the slow lane, trying not to attract attention. Fortunately, the Merc had tinted side windows which camouflaged his youthful appearance.

'My hero,' Carly giggled excitedly, trying to forget the seriousness of their situation. But the moment was short lived, as they heard a siren sound behind them.

'It's the Police,' announced Derek, checking his rearview mirror. 'Hold on Carly. We'll have to make a run for it!' Derek put his foot to the floor and the Mercedes shot forward. But the siren was still hot on their tail.

'It's useless, Derek,' Carly murmured resignedly.

'No!' Derek insisted, as he continued to skid all over the road.

The Police were now alongside him but Derek had spotted a side exit ahead and again he put his foot to the floor. However, his lack of driving experience showed, as the car spun out of control, skidding sideways. Carly screamed as all Derek's efforts failed to stop them from crashing into the police car beside them.

At the Police Station, both Carly and Derek were charged.

'Just be grateful that no one was hurt,' the desk Sergeant suggested as he showed them to the waiting area. 'I'm sure your parents will be grateful for that!' he added with a wry smile as he left Carly and Derek sitting alone.

'I'm so sorry, Derek,' Carly stammered. 'If it wasn't for me, you wouldn't be in this mess.

'Hey, Carly, forget it! What are friends for . . . right?' Derek assured her with a smile. Carly took Derek's hand, smiling her own appreciation. 'Besides, I'm sure something good can come out of all this,' Derek added optimistically.

But no sooner were his words out, than Carly looked up and saw the figure of her father standing in front of them.

'Yes Sergeant, that's my daughter,' George confirmed to the Police Officer beside him. 'I'll take her home now if that's alright?' Carly's face dropped.

'But Carly must be back in juvenile court on Monday morning at 9 a.m. Mr Morris,' the Sergeant advised, as George and Carly left. George nodded. But the last thing in the world he wanted was his daughter in a Courtroom, blurting out to the world that her father had killed her mother. If anyone ever started to believe her story, he could kiss his business and professional standing goodbye.

'There must be a way out' George thought desperately to himself on the car ride home. He had hardly noticed Carly, he was so consumed by his own sticky position. But as they pulled up in front of the house again, he suddenly saw the girl stiffen and he read the terror which was written all over her face.

chapter five

In exchange for a fair compensation payment to the police department and a dropping of the charges against Derek Peterson, George managed to have Carly's required court appearance substituted by a group of guidance sessions with a Social Worker. Carly's case was to be reviewed according to the findings of that Social Worker in six months' time. The same rules applied to Derek although neither George nor Carly knew of this fact.

George was relieved. If he could keep Carly out of the public eye for the time being, he was convinced the girl would eventually be broken and give up on this vendetta she waged against him.

But Carly was required to attend the sessions with the Social Worker in the city, rather than at home. George requested a review of this but to no avail. It troubled him that his

rebellious daughter would be out of his juris-
diction, out of his control. But his hands
were tied.

The Social Worker assigned to Carly's case was
Tarquin Pierce who was young and brash but
completely diligent at his work. He could spot a
phoney a mile off and George Morris had rung
alarm bells with him from the first time they'd
met. George had thrust Carly's psychiatric
report at Tarquin in an attempt to undermine
the girl's credibility. And then he had mentioned the lawyers he could enlist to help if
Carly's case was ever foolishly reassigned to
juvenile court. If things were to go the wrong
way, George had intimated that he could make
life very unpleasant for a lowly social worker
such as Pierce. But Tarquin was not so easily
intimidated. He banned George from his sessions with Carly and announced that his own
findings would reflect the situation as he saw
it. 'In other words, go to hell, Morris, or I'll be
forced to have you charged with tampering
with the legal process!' Tarquin had said, as he
closed the door in George's face.

From his first interview with Carly, Tarquin
was convinced by her story and incensed by
the treatment she had received in the wake
of her mother's death.

'I'll get you out of that house! Don't you worry, Carly,' he'd consoled her.

During the week that followed, Tarquin moved quickly. His third session with Carly was scheduled for Friday morning and he wanted everything to be ready. He requested that George attend this session, that way the papers could be signed and Carly could be out of that torture chamber she'd been living in before the weekend was over.

Tarquin asked Carly to wait outside while he spoke to George Morris alone. He was repulsed by this man, who had waged such physical and psychological abuse upon Carly, so he wasted no time in placing his cards on the table.

'For Carly's own safety, I've recommended her removal from your home,' Tarquin said, looking George straight in the eye. For a moment the older man was stunned. 'The way I see it, Morris,' Tarquin continued, 'you have two choices. You can give up your harrassment of Carly and allow her to be made of ward of the court without putting up a fight, in which case the girl would be fostered to a family of the court's choosing. Or,' he paused, 'or, you can fight for the return of your daughter which would result in a lengthy court battle. And if you choose to fight in court, Morris, I must warn you now, I'll hold nothing back. I'll dig up all the dirt I can find on you. And one way, or another, the public will be made aware of your actions.'

'You can't prove anything, Pierce,' George interrupted anxiously.

'Proof? Oh ... but proof isn't the issue, Morris,' Tarquin laughed. 'I'm sure you could weazle out of just about anything. But while you can wipe off the mud, it always leaves a stain. And that's what your type is terrified of, Morris. Your standing in the community would be shot to ribbons. You see, there'd always be that lingering doubt in everyone's mind . . .'

'I was cleared of any responsibility for my wife's death,' George snapped defensively.

'Yes,' Tarquin agreed, with a wry smile. 'But if a further case were to be brought against you for the brutalization of your daughter ... well ... it might just renew interest in that earlier incident. And I've no doubt, you'd be on the front pages of all the leading newspapers, Morris, for all the wrong reasons!'

Beads of perspiration had gathered on George Morris's forehead and one of his eyelids twitched nervously. Tarquin was sure he had him. 'Well?' he asked George, matter-of-factly.

'OK! OK! Take the brat!' George said, defeatedly, with a halting gesture of his hand. 'But no publicity! No further publicity. That's my only condition.'

'Sign here,' Tarquin said, cooly, pushing the official documents towards George.

Carly remained with Tarquin for the rest of the day. She was overjoyed by the prospect of leaving home. But she baulked at the 'no further publicity' condition.

'No,' she shrieked, 'he can't get away with that!'

'Carly, you have to let go. There's no other way out,' Tarquin counselled.

By lunchtime, Derek had arrived.

'You've been having sessions with Tarquin too?' Carly queried, in disbelief.

'Yes,' Derek confirmed. 'It was a condition of my release from the charges.'

'You've certainly found a true friend in Derek, Carly,' Tarquin said.

'I know,' Carly readily agreed, as she threw Derek a broad affectionate grin.

'He helped corroborate your story,' Tarquin explained. 'That way I was able to get things moving much more quickly.' Have you thought more about your father's condition, Carly?' he asked.

'Do you know about the publicity ban that Dad's insisted upon?' Carly anxiously asked Derek.

The boy nodded. 'It's time to turn over a new leaf, Carly,' Derek said, placing a comforting arm around her.

'But that means that both Dad and Samantha would get off scott-free,' Carly reiterated. 'It's not fair . . . it's just not fair!'

'I know, Carly,' Tarquin consoled. 'But in order to survive yourself, you'll just have to accept that life isn't always fair. We all do our best but the guilty aren't always brought to justice.'

'Yes,' Derek agreed. 'And this bitterness is just eating you away, Carly.'

She looked at the two faces pleading with

her. They had both been through a lot to help her. Derek had even risked his own life in that car-chase.

'Alright!' she said, suddenly breaking the silence. 'I'm not happy about it. But, alright, I'll play by the rules.'

She saw the relief on their faces and felt Derek's arm squeeze her tightly. She just hoped that she wouldn't regret this decision some time in the future.

On Sunday afternoon, Tarquin picked Carly up from the house. She'd packed everything of importance into two suitcases and simply walked out the front door. No one had said goodbye. There had been no last moment threats. Not long after, Derek had jumped into the car beside her, and together the trio had driven off towards Carly's new home.

'The Fletchers are a warm and caring couple,' Tarquin explained as he drove. 'They already have another foster child, Frank. But as he'll be seventeen on his next birthday, they felt it was time to take on another charge.'

'And that's me!' Carly said, stating the obvious, as she held Derek's hand tightly.

'And that's you,' Tarquin echoed.

A mixture of thoughts swam about in Carly's head. She had no idea what to expect. But she was sure whatever lay ahead, it would be an improvement on what she'd left behind.

'Well, here we are,' Tarquin suddenly announced as he swung the car towards a modest-looking terrace house with a large tree in the front yard. Carly felt the butterflies flutter in her stomach.

The Fletchers appeared as they heard the car arrive. 'Hello, I'm Pippa and this is my husband, Tom,' the petite blond woman said by way of introduction as her husband waved and smiled. 'We're very pleased to meet you, Carly.'

'Hello,' Carly replied, a little stiffly, as the group was ushered into the house. But as she took in her surroundings, Carly began to have doubts. Everything looked so makeshift. Surely there had been some mistake. Tarquin wasn't going to leave her here, in this run-down house.

'And this will be your room,' Pippa said as she helped Carly along the hall with her bags. They walked into a room that reminded Carly of an oversized cupboard. She was lost for words. She'd always had all the comforts money could buy. This was quite a come-down.

But later, as she waved goodbye to Tarquin and Derek, Carly maintained a brave front. She'd have to weather this place at least for now. After all, her choices were somewhat limited. And the Fletchers weren't too bad, even though they were working-class people.

Three days later, Carly began classes at the local high school. She was amazed, not only by the huge number of students attending the school, but also by the mixture of per-sonalities she found in the corridors. Her days at boarding school and at the private academy she'd attended with Samantha hadn't come anywhere near preparing her for the experience of a Government School. At first, she'd tried to keep a low profile. But as 'the new girl', no one had let her get away with that. To Carly, some of the kids seemed really rough; and then there were the dirty ones; and then just the disgusting ones. She found the going tough. She wasn't fitting in and she knew it. More and more,

Carly felt the need to state her superiority in this alien environment.

'Yes, my mother was "the" Susan Morris. You've probably heard of her. She was a world-class model,' Carly boasted to a group of class-mates with whom she'd been assigned to do a history project.

'God, you think you're such a toff, Morris,' a boy with a pimple-ridden face scoffed at Carly. 'But you're no better than us and it's about time you realized it!' The group finished the project without her help.

As her 'new girl' status began to wear off, Carly found more and more that she was avoided by the other kids at school. Initially, she preferred it that way. But as she sat alone at lunchtime and at the back of the classroom for most of her subjects, the feeling of deep unhappiness again swamped her.

Derek arrived one weekend, completely un-announced, to find Carly moping in her bedroom.

'I hate it here,' she confided to him. 'I mean, look at this dump, Derek. I just don't fit in.'

'You've got to give things a chance, Carly,' he consoled. 'After all, you've only been here a month. You have to expect a period of adjustment.'

'No! Nothing's going to change,' Carly replied dismally. 'Oh, please, Derek, can't I come and live with you and your Dad? I'd be no trouble – really I wouldn't,' she added, with tears welling in her eyes.

'Carly, it wouldn't work,' Derek said, gently. 'Don't you see, you have to live with a family appointed by the Youth and Community Services. That's the law.'

'But maybe the department could appoint your father to foster me,' Carly pleaded.

'Well, actually, Carly,' Derek hesitated, 'Dad's just landed a contract with one of the major European fashion houses,' he explained, as he placed his arm around her, trying to brace her for his news. 'That's why I've come to see you. You see, we'll be leaving for Europe in two weeks.'

'Leaving?' Carly queried, despondently.

'Yes ... I don't know how long we'll be gone. Months or maybe even years, I suppose,' Derek stammered as he watched the distress spread across Carly's face. 'But it won't be forever, Carly. I'll be back, I promise.'

Carly tried to hide her disappointment. She hugged Derek to her, telling him how happy she was for him. But the only thought that ran through her mind was that the only friend she had in the world was deserting her.

As she waved goodbye to Derek at the airport a fortnight later, Carly began to form her plan. It wouldn't be so difficult. Plenty of kids did it every year; and got away with it, according to the newspaper stories she'd read. She'd simply run away and disappear into the city. She still had a little money of her own in a bank account not even her father had ever known about. It would be enough to give her a start anyway. No one would ever find her. She could simply vanish and forget all about her father, the Youth and Community Services and the boringly suburban and cloying Fletchers.

Carly watched as Derek's plane climbed higher and finally disappeared into a cloud bank. Yes, she'd have to get away on her own. That was her answer.

chapter six

Tom drove Carly back home after her airport farewell with Derek. She sat silently throughout the journey.

'You don't have much to say, do you?' Tom asked kindly. He and Pippa had felt the girl's growing resentment of her situation at home with them.

'No, not much,' Carly replied curtly.

Tom prided himself on being able to read people well. He knew everything about Carly's family turmoil, but still he'd been unable to crack the shell into which the girl had withdrawn. Nothing he and Pippa did had worked. Carly was always so sullen. He'd never even seen the girl smile. She was a hard one but Tom was determined to keep trying.

Carly was relieved when they'd arrived back home. She didn't feel up to fielding any questions from Tom. She quickly disappeared to her room and began packing. After dinner, when the house was quiet, she planned to slip out her bedroom window; it wouldn't take long to reach the city where there were always cheap boarding houses. And tomorrow she could begin her new life. But first, she'd have to quietly fill these suitcases. She lifted her second bag down from the top of the peeling wardrobe, the one Tom had promised to repaint for her this coming weekend. But Carly tried not to think about promises. She busied herself with folding clothes.

Pippa Fletcher sat at the kitchen table, sensing that her time was running out with Carly.

'Hi, Pippa,' Frank said brightly as he walked into the room. But then he noticed the solemn look on Pippa's face. 'Something wrong?' he queried.

'Frank! Maybe you can help.' Pippa said hopefully.

'If I can,' Frank said amiably. 'What's up?'

'Frank, when you first came to us . . . and you had that time when you felt so alienated, can you remember something – anything –

that helped you to adjust?' Pippa asked anxiously. Frank looked puzzled for a while. 'Anything at all, Frank,' Pippa urged. 'You see, I think we're failing with Carly and I just don't know what else to try.'

Suddenly, Frank's face brightened. 'I know,' he exclaimed, enthusiastically. 'It was the photo! when you took that family snap – that welcome to the family photo of all of us together. I'd never had a photo like that before. I felt I was really a part of your family then . . .'

Pippa jumped up, smiling, and kissed him. 'Thanks,' she whispered, as she ran off to find Tom.

The knock on Carly's door surprised her. She quickly pushed the half-filled suitcase under her bed before she called 'Come in!'

'Carly, could you come out to the kitchen for a moment please?' Pippa asked as she stuck her head in.

'What for?' Carly queried.

'You'll see,' Pippa replied mysteriously with a smile.

*

Before she realized it, Carly had been piled into the car with Frank, Tom and Pippa. They stopped at the local park and Tom began to set up the camera.

'It's a family tradition,' shrugged Frank when questioned by a perplexed Carly.

'OK. Everyone smile!' Tom ordered as the automatic camera captured the four of them on film.

Pippa placed a caring arm around Carly as she took her off for a stroll through the park.

'We wanted to capture us all together in a photo as sort of a way of saying to the world that we're a family,' Pippa explained to Carly as they walked. 'I want us to be bonded together as people, like our images are in that photo,' Pippa continued. 'I don't want to replace your mother in your life, darling. I know how much you loved her. But maybe, if you'll let us, Tom and I can make up for some of the hurt you've experienced. What do you think, Carly?'

Carly shrugged. 'I don't know ... maybe,' she murmured, feeling very confused.

'Look, I know the house and everything are a far cry from what you've been used to in life. But . . . well, there's nothing we can do to change that,' Pippa said honestly. 'But, we can give you lots of love and support . . . if you'll let us. We really do want to help you, darling. At least, think about it, will you?' she added, as they rejoined Tom and Frank. Carly nodded, as she looked up into Pippa's gentle open face.

When Tom called her for dinner that night, Carly still didn't know what to do. But as she sat down to the table, Pippa caught her glance and smiled. Instinctively, Carly smiled back. Pippa's warmth and honesty were very persuasive. Suddenly, Carly noticed that the kitchen had a sort of rustic-charm about it that she'd missed before. The food tasted great too. She hadn't realised how hungry she was. And when Tom mentioned he'd bought the paint to fix up her wardrobe on the weekend. She smiled again. That old peeling wardrobe could certainly do with a face-lift!

Across the table, Tom and Pippa exchanged a knowing look of relief. Perhaps they had crossed the first hurdle with Carly. Although they still had a long way to go, things might just begin to improve from here on in. And, in between the tinkle of cutlery and the passing of bread, the seed of hope started to sprout.

Back in her room, after dinner, Carly unpacked her bags. Running away had been marked off her agenda for tonight or any night. She knew now she could make things work. She'd try harder. She had a family to help her and that was something new for her. Somehow, she'd changed her outlook since this morning. Even her room didn't look too bad now, she decided with a grin, thinking how much better her wardrobe would look after its trendy colour change.

It was another six months before Derek returned home for a visit. He longed to see Carly and wasted no time in arriving on her doorstep.

'I can't believe it,' he said to her, after they'd finished lunch with the family. 'You've really changed. You're just so happy. I thought your letters sounded positive. But in person, well, look at you, you blow my mind!'

'Thanks,' Carly said delightedly. 'And what do you think of this?' she asked, as she produced the latest 'welcome to the family' photo. Tom and Pippa's family had extended even more to include Lynn who had been a constant runaway, and Sally, a little girl whose grandmother had become too senile to look after her.

Derek surveyed the photo closely. The six members of the family all looked happy. But he was sure that Carly shone out brightest of all. 'It's great!' he assured her, as he noticed she had an extra copy in her hand. 'What's the extra copy for?' he asked.

'Well, if you come with me, you'll soon find out,' Carly replied mysteriously, as she slipped the extra photo into an envelope.

As the taxi pulled up outside Carly's father's house, Derek began to worry. Carly paid the fare and let the driver go.

'Carly, come on. Why are we here?' Derek questioned.

'I've come to get my revenge on Dad and Samantha . . . at last!' Carly replied as she gazed up at the house.

Derek felt his heart begin to race. He couldn't believe it. He'd been so sure she was through with all that. Then he looked into Carly's face. She looked so serene. She smiled at him and suddenly all his worries disappeared. He watched her as she took out the envelope containing the photo and slipped it into her father's mailbox.

'There,' she said with a sigh. 'It's done!'

'What's done?' Derek asked, still bewildered.

'My revenge,' Carly announced with satisfaction. 'I've accomplished my revenge.'

But Derek still looked puzzled. 'Don't you see, Derek?' Carly patiently explained. 'When they look at that photo, they'd have to be blind not to see how happy I am. And there's nothing they can do to change it! Not a thing in the world. Now what better revenge could there be?' she added with a laugh. And then Derek laughed too, as he finally understood.

Just as the sun was beginning to set on the city skyline, Carly and Derek walked hand-in-hand down the street and away from the house. Carly inhaled the crisp twilight air with relish. She felt so vital, so alive. Suddenly, the world seemed such a wonderful place to her, and the future shone out like a beacon, beckoning her forward. And with joy, the realisation dawned upon Carly that she had finally exorcised the ghosts of her past.

THE
Steven Matheson
STORY

FANTAIL

chapter one

Past the Henderson's border-beds of flowers
and the Jackson's line of pencil pines, the
thin weedy boy ran on towards the sanctuary of his own home.

'I'll get you Matheson!' a breathless voice
called out from somewhere behind him.
But Steven continued to run, not daring to
look back at the larger boy who pursued
him. Old Mr Henery glanced up from his
verandah, a little bewildered, as Steven
pounded by, giving the old man a wave and
a smile.

'He must think I'm off the planet,' the boy
thought to himself, as he read the astonish-
ment on the old man's face. Then he heard
Jock Barry's voice boom out again: 'Come
back and fight Matheson, you gutless
wonder!'

But Steven never faltered. Jock was built like
a granite mountain. The smaller boy knew

all he had to do was to head for home: Jock would never catch him. And, as Steven retreated towards the safety of home, the events which led him into his current predicament flashed through his head.

It had all started with Tracey Oldman. Steven had known Tracey almost since kindergarten. But suddenly, she was different. She'd always been OK, for a girl; someone he'd tolerated. But lately, he'd noticed things about her that were new. Like her smile and her hair. Not forgetting her body! She looked like someone from a TV series or a rock band. Over the years, she'd become a real spunk and, although at fourteen she was a year older than Steven, he'd decided to ask her out on a date. Kevin Harris had dared him to do it. So he had. Everyone knew that Tracey was Jock Barry's girlfriend but Steven figured it was time for Tracey to reconsider her position. After all, apart from Jock's towering stature, and the fact that he was sixteen years old and could dip into his family's wealth whenever he wanted, what did the big bully really have going for him? Jock had made most of the friends he had at school by his intimidation tactics. Kids were scared of his physical strength and so they'd decided it was safer to be with him than against him. Maybe Tracey had felt that way too, Steven had decided. If he gave her a chance, perhaps she could re-evaluate and choose him instead. It was worth a try anyway.

Steven had imagined asking Tracey out a hundred times over in his head. He'd practised his lines as though he was rehearsing a part for a play. And in these mental rehearsals, Tracey had always said 'yes'. But when the real thing had gone down, her reaction was a far cry from that which Steven had visualized.

'Go out with you, Stevie?' Tracey had queried in disbelief.

Steven had nodded, feeling all eyes upon him and noting Tracey's use of the childish name, 'Stevie'.

'You mean on a date?' Tracey had repeated.

'Yes,' Steven had confirmed as he looked up into her big blue eyes. 'I thought we could go to a movie or maybe you'd prefer dinner somewhere?' he'd added, noticing smirks beginning to break out on the faces of Tracey's circle of friends.

'I see,' Tracey had said with sarcasm in her

voice. 'And what time would I have to have you home by?' she'd asked with a dead pan look.

There was a rush of unbridled laughter from the circle. Steven could feel the blood rushing to his face.

'I,' he paused with an emphasis on the word, 'would get you home by your usual curfew!' he had announced, trying to cover his embarrassment.

'Well, I think all the "general exhibition" movies let out fairly early,' Tracey had quipped with a laugh as Steven's heart sank. 'I think maybe you're out of your league, here, Stevie. Try me again in a few years' time, eh?' she'd added, as the circle seemed to rock with amusement, before breaking open to allow Jock Barry through.

'What's going on here, Matheson?' Jock had questioned. But before Steven could answer, Tracey had hastily intervened.

'Nothing, Jock,' she said, as she threw Steven a concerned look. 'Stevie's just testing his wings, that's all,' she'd added, linking her arm through Jock's.

But Jock Barry had heard exactly what was

going on. And he didn't like it. He didn't like it one bit!

'How is it a little weed like you, Matheson, thinks he can ask my girl out behind my back?' Jock had asked Steven, unlinking himself from Tracey and grabbing the smaller boy by the shirtfront.

Steven had realized his situation but he just couldn't hold back his reply.

'Maybe I thought she was starved for some intellectual stimulation,' he'd snapped.

'You razzing me, Matheson?' Jock had questioned as he began to shake Steven, threateningly. 'You sayin' I'm dumb?'

'No,' Steven had replied with an innocent smile. Jock slackened his hold a little, looking confused.

'Not dumb,' Steven assured him. 'Neanderthal is a more fitting word for a big ape like you!' he yelled as he wriggled loose and took flight. An incensed Jock Barry was soon in hot pursuit, ready to spread one Steven Matheson across the pavement.

If only he'd used his head and kept his big mouth shut, Steven now thought to himself, as he pounded along the pavement: Maybe he wouldn't be in this sticky situation. But his sharp tongue often led him into confrontation; confrontation from which his nimble speed usually supplied him with his means of escape. But it was a hot day and the boy was grateful to at last come to the corner and turn into his own street. He wasn't so pleased to see his father just arriving home in the family car with the 'Matheson Karate School' logo, so clearly displayed on its door. He just hoped Jock Barry wouldn't spot that. He didn't need anyone taunting him with 'karate kid' insinuations.

Steven jumped the front fence, giving his father his customary 'Hi Dad' wave as he headed up on to the verandah of the house. Perhaps if he maintained a cool air, his father wouldn't notice his situation. Or maybe Jock wouldn't even make it this far; maybe the big ape had given up back near Mr Henery's place. 'Wrong again!' Steven mentally noted, as he glanced towards the corner of the street to see a panting and breathless Jock Barry just then come into view. At the sight of Steven's father in the front yard, Jock abruptly halted. Teasingly, Steven gave Jock a wave and a smile. The older boy glared back and raised a threatening fist into the air. But Steven continued to smile, until Jock's defeated figure turned and walked slowly back around the corner. It was only then that Steven looked in the direction of his father who had been standing and watching the whole scene unfold.

Brett Matheson shut the garage door with extra force. He couldn't understand his son's behaviour. Why would Steven run away from someone like that Barry kid? A brown belt in karate, Steven could easily have overcome an opponent such as Jock Barry. It was time to have a father-to-son talk with Steven, Brett decided, as he followed Steven's retreating figure through the front door and into the house.

'Surely you know you could cream someone like that Barry kid, Steven!' Brett exclaimed to his son, as they both reached the kitchen.

'But I didn't want to cream him, Dad,' Steven explained, a little irritated.

'But son, self-defence . . .' Brett began.

'Only fight when you have no other recourse,' Steven interrupted. 'That's the basic maxim of karate; you taught it to me yourself, Dad!'

'Yes, but running away isn't what I judge to

be "another recourse"!' Brett Matheson snapped, becoming a little exasperated. Steven had apparently taken the philosophy of karate very much to heart – a little too literally as far as Brett was concerned.

'I mean, well what was the use of you becoming so skilled in karate if you're never going to be prepared to use it?' Brett questioned. But Steven merely shrugged. Then it hit Brett that maybe Steven had kept his karate training a secret. Perhaps none of his friends was even aware of Steven's skills.

'So no one at school knows you've had karate training!' Brett queried watching the truth of his statement reflected in Steven's face.

'No!' came Steven's short and honest reply. Brett's face fell with disappointment.

'What . . . you're ashamed of the fact! And I suppose you're ashamed that karate is the means by which I earn my living!' Brett accused his son, his strained voice conveying his own inner pain and hurt.

'It's not like that, Dad,' Steven said sympathetically, placing his arm on his father's shoulder. 'Come on, I'm not ashamed. I'm very proud that you're an instructor. But I

do karate for me – for my own inner self –
not so I can pose off in front of everyone at
school,' he added as Brett sat down at the
table and Steven took the opposite seat. 'If
the kids at school knew, Dad,' Steven continued, 'I'd probably have to face up to every
jerk who needed to test himself against
"Matheson the Mighty". And that's something I want to avoid. To me, karate is more
than just some weapon I can use to impress
people with. It gives me a feeling of control,
a sense of worth.' Steven looked into his
father's eyes, but the hurt was still there. Brett
Matheson sat mute. 'I know I could have
taken out Jock Barry, Dad. And that's the
"power" of karate: knowing I could have
done him. That's all that counts as far as I'm
concerned,' Steven added, becoming frus-
trated by his father's lack of understanding.

'You can't run away forever, son. That's all
I'm saying!' Brett told Steven gruffly, as he
left to go upstairs. The boy sat on alone in
the kitchen, feeling that although a gulf of
misunderstanding now separated him from
his father, the older man would eventually
come around to see things his way. Later
that night, however, this belief began to
dim.

*

Steven was in his own room, lying in bed, when the murmuring which had been coming from his parents' bedroom suddenly erupted into a shouting match.

'And I love him too, Alice!' his father's voice boomed. 'But Steven has to grow up. He can't go on running away from confrontation.'

'He did the right thing, Brett,' Alice Matheson shouted back at her husband. 'Just because he isn't following in your footsteps, doesn't make him wrong, you know. Sensitivity is nothing to be ashamed of!'

Steven put his hands over his ears. But still his father's voice filtered into his head: 'All I'm saying is that you can take this "turn the other cheek" stuff too far.'

A flat, empty feeling seemed to settle inside Steven. 'When you were little you could cry when you felt like this,' he told himself. But at thirteen, Steven felt he no longer had the luxury of crying like a baby. All he could do now was to turn over and try to sleep. Perhaps a new day would bring clarity to this confusing situation.

As the voices from the other room faded, Steven Matheson slipped into an uneasy sleep.

chapter two

'Anyone home?' came a call from the back door. Steven made his way from the front of the house to find his Uncle Philip already standing inside the kitchen.

'Hi, Steve! How's it going?' Philip asked, giving his favourite nephew a playful box around the ears.

'Goodday, Uncle Phil,' Steven said, feeling a sudden surge of happiness at the sight of Philip. 'I thought you were on duty at the hospital all this week. How come you're here?'

'One of the other residents needed a swap of shifts, so I obliged,' Philip answered. 'And I found myself with an hour or so free so I thought I'd catch up on family news. Where is my big brother, anyway?'

'Dad went down to the Karate School early. There's a load of new matting arriving. And Mum's gone to town for the day,' Steven

113

explained as he passed Philip a long strong black coffee.

'Thanks, mate,' Philip said, gratefully slurping into the coffee. But he looked at Steven, noticing his favourite nephew was uncharacteristically despondent this morning. 'What's up?' he asked with genuine concern.

Steven was reluctant to bring someone else into his dilemma. But then Uncle Phil was not just 'someone else'. And after some extra coaxing from Philip, Steven told him of his problem.

'So if I stand up and fight, it'll keep Dad happy. But it's not what I really want to do. I mean I don't really think it's the right way of handling things,' Steven said seriously.

'Well, sounds as if this Jock Barry is someone that needs to be cut down to size,' Philip commented.

'Oh, yes, he does,' agreed Steven. 'It's just that I don't know if I should be the one to wield the axe,' he added, still a little confused by his own quandary.

Philip looked into the frowning face of his nephew.

'I can't see your problem, Steve. If this big ox is picking on you, just take him out and be done with it!' Philip advised with a laugh. 'I think you're taking all this too seriously, if you ask me!' he added light-heartedly as he munched on some toast.

Steven envied his Uncle Philip. Nothing ever seemed to be 'too serious' in Philip's life. His happy-go-lucky attitude was one Steven admired.

Suddenly, the sound of an air-horn from outside on the driveway pierced the relative calm of the Matheson house.

'Oh! Got to bale, kid. That'll be Justine!' Philip said as he grabbed his coat and downed the remainder of his second cup of coffee.

'Justine?' Steven asked. 'What about Louise?'

'That was last week, Steve,' Philip explained with a wink. 'Variety is the spice of life, you know,' he laughed as Steven followed him out to the waiting sports car on the driveway.

Philip climbed into the red sports car, giving Steven some final encouragement.

'Now go get that big bully, tiger,' he commanded over the purr of the engine. 'And lighten up a little, hey?'

'I'll try,' Steven promised, as he waved goodbye to his zany Uncle. 'Maybe Philip was right,' he thought as he watched the red sports car wind its way out of the street. He was taking all this pretty seriously. Why ... his father might have already forgotten all about it and they could start with a clean slate. 'Lighten up!' he ordered himself aloud as he grabbed his books for school. He'd just go to his scheduled karate class after school and act as though nothing had happened, he decided. That would be the way to play it!

But later that afternoon, at the karate school, it didn't take Steven too long to realize that his planned 'clean slate' tactic wasn't going to work. His father was leading the class Steven was taking, and pushing his son harder than all the others.

'Is this beyond you, Matheson?' Brett asked his son for the third time. Steven felt the eyes of the class upon him, as he shook his head solemnly. His father had belittled him almost from the moment he'd entered the room. The boy knew that this niggling commentary was in some way linked to his father's disappointment in him, but it was beginning to wear him down. Finally, in demonstrating a throw, Brett called upon Steven's assistance. But in front of the class, Brett again criticized his son and Steven's patience suddenly snapped.

Steven sprang to his feet and lashed out at his father, hoping to humiliate him by throwing him in front of the class, thereby giving him a taste of his own sour medicine. But the boy underestimated the older man's excellent reflexes. Brett Matheson was a black belt and had justly earned his position as instructor. As a result, Steven found himself once more on the floor, staring up at the ceiling.

'And that's a good example of how not to make that throw,' Brett said to the class, and Steven felt he wanted to dig a hole and crawl in.

Once the class was over, Steven wasted no time in leaving the karate school. The more distance he could place between himself and his father, the better as far as he was concerned. He headed for the park. The sun was just beginning to set and it was the time of day that the boy liked best. But not even the twilight, with all its soft inviting magic, would lift Steven's spirits right now. He sat beneath the largest tree in the park, mulling over the events of the past couple of days. The trouble between himself and his father was gnawing at him. He was divided between bitterness, anger, frustration and love. He not only wanted his father's understanding and approval; there was a part of him that really needed it. The boy stood up, kicking listlessly at the base of the tree. He wanted to cry. But he steeled himself against tears. Tears were for little kids. Instead, his small but wiry figure swept into his routine of centreing exercises. Over a period of years now, his concentration and balance had been finely honed through his practice of these karate movements. He blocked the world out by using rigid concentration to mentally cleanse his inner mind of all its emotional grime. The fluid movement of his small frame testified to his long years of practice. But he almost totally lost everything, as the figure of his father moved into his line of controlled vision. He steadied himself from breaking his focus; he merely ignored his father and continued his routine, knowing that his father's own respect for karate would never allow him to intrude.

*

Brett Matheson waited. He watched his son with admiration. Steven had clearly learnt well. And as Steven finished and turned to face his father, Brett noticed a change in the face of his son. The anger and hostility with which Steven had been fuelled earlier in the afternoon had been replaced by a calm tranquility.

'We need to talk, son,' Brett announced quietly.

Steven nodded and took up his seat beneath the tree. Brett sat down beside him and they both stared out into the dimming twilight.

'First, I should explain,' Brett began, 'that I agree with you: there is no joy to be found in fighting.' Brett paused as Steven looked up into his father's eyes and a recognition of sympathy and understanding passed between them. 'But,' Brett continued, 'there is honour to be found in self-defence. Even the most peaceful of people can be faced, at some time in their lives, with the need to defend themselves. And by running away, they will only make themselves weaker and the bullies of this world stronger,' Brett added before Steven could interrupt.

'So what you're saying is that Jock Barry will only gather more strength because no one is prepared to stand up to him?' Steven queried.

'Yes,' Brett agreed. 'You said yourself, he has the whole school intimidated. How do you think he gathered that sort of power?' Brett asked as Steven nodded, thinking of all the kids at school who bowed and scraped to Jock because they were too scared of what he might do to them otherwise.

'You see, son,' Brett continued, placing an arm on Steven's shoulder, 'to have someone run away, gives the bully more to crow about. Jock Barry probably thinks he's invincible – that's how it works, while the peaceful person stews in his own anger. And anger and self-doubt are negative emotions which will knock down the peaceful one just as effectively as the intimidating bully could have done,' Brett paused, hoping his message was sinking in. 'When you lashed out at me today, Steven,' Brett said, as his son averted his gaze, 'you were ineffective because you were angry. You attempted to floor me to fulfil your own negative needs, not from a more honorable emotion. And when a person fights in anger, they have much less chance of winning.'

Steven knew the truth of this remark and was suddenly remorseful.

'I'll leave you to absorb all of this, son,' Brett added as he rose to his feet, giving Steven a light pat on the head. 'I'm just glad I've had the chance to explain. But now it's your decision, Steven,' Brett paused, glancing up at the darkening sky, 'and I always thought that this was the best time of day to make decisions,' he added with a smile as he slowly walked away.

Steven watched his father's figure until it merged with the dimness that was the approaching night and he could see it no more. The wisdom of his words echoed in Steven's head and the boy realized that he had misjudged his father. Suddenly, Steven felt that the gulf that had separated them from one another had disappeared. Father and son had again been joined together by the bridge of understanding. A smile broke over Steven's face. In a way, he was glad all this had happened as he had never before felt this close to his father. He rose to his feet, feeling a new part of his life was about to begin.

But little did he realize that he would never have the chance to tell his father this good news!

chapter three

Steven walked out of the park and headed for home. He breathed in the cooler air of evening with relish.

'Hey Steve! Wait up!' came a voice from somewhere in the dark behind him. Steven turned around to see Danny Graham emerge from the shadow of semi-darkness. Danny and his family lived across the street from the Mathesons and the two boys were long-time mates.

'Hi, Danny. Going home?' Steven asked, as his friend caught him up.

'Yeh. I've just been down the sports store for some extra sinkers,' Danny explained, indicating the bag he was carrying. 'Dad and me are going fishin' tomorrow morning, up Scaler's River.'

'Sounds great!' Steven said, as they continued walking.

'Well, why don't you come too?' Danny asked, suddenly more excited.

A smile of delight spread across Steven's face.

'But wouldn't your Dad mind?' he asked tentatively.

'Course not!' Danny declared.

'OK. Then I'd love to,' Steven agreed, as the pair smartened their pace, spurred on by the added anticipation.

'We're leaving at five in the morning, so we can get into the really big ones,' Danny chuckled. 'So it'd be better if you came over for dinner and then stayed the night at our house, Steve. OK?'

'OK. I'll clear the decks at home first and see you for dinner then,' Steven confirmed as he waved goodbye at his front gate.

'And don't forget your fishing gear,' Danny reminded him, as he disappeared into the darkness across the street.

Steven walked into his house, noticing that it looked somehow different. Then he realized that the difference was the security grilles that had been newly attached to all the windows.

'Mum?' he called, as he closed the front door.

'In the kitchen,' came Alice Matheson's reply.

Steven found his mother, still dressed in her 'going to town' clothes, sitting with a tradesman at the kitchen table.

'Mr Hooper is just drawing up our account for the new security grilles,' his mother explained to Steven. The boy looked out through the grille on the kitchen window.

'We're behind bars, Mum,' he commented. 'It's like we're prisoners in our own home,' he added with a touch of theatrical melodrama. And although he didn't realize it at the time, this remark was later to echo in Steven's head with added meaning.

'Well, it's better to install security grilles than to be robbed of everything like the Coopers were last week,' his mother reminded him, while making awkward faces behind Mr Hooper's back. Obviously his mother thought that Mr Hooper might be offended by Steven's jokes about his security-grille business. His mother was like that. She was right about the Coopers though – they were neighbours from down the street who'd come home one night to find their house totally empty. And theirs was just one of the many neighbourhood robberies the police were still investigating.

While Mr Hooper was still calculating costs, Steven hastily explained to his mother of his proposed fishing trip with Danny. After receiving her OK, he then raced upstairs, packed his gear and started off for Danny's house.

'Tell Dad I'll see him tomorrow arvo, will you Mum?' he asked as he kissed his mother goodbye. She smiled approvingly at him, realizing her son and his father must have patched things up. 'And we'll be expecting fish for dinner then,' she added with a laugh, as Steven, in a clatter of rods and landing nets, disappeared through the kitchen door.

Later that night, after having enjoyed a leisurely dinner with the Grahams, Danny and Steven decided to catch an early movie at the local theatre. While waiting in line to buy their tickets, Steven caught sight of Tracey Oldman who was standing alone by the candy counter. Before he could decide whether or not to play it cool and ignore her, she had spotted him and was coming over.

'Hi, Steve. Hi, Danny,' Tracey said amiably, as Danny gave Steven an elbow in the side. Danny knew just how much Steven liked Tracey and the 'friendly' elbowing was his signal to his mate to turn on the charm.

'Hi, Tracey. Here alone?' Danny asked, as he jabbed Steven again, pushing him forward a little. Danny was a born match-maker.

'Yes,' Tracey replied, as she glanced around, 'Jock was s'posed to be here but looks like he's stood me up!' she observed with a touch of irritation in her voice.

'You go talk to Tracey and I'll get the tickets, Steve,' Danny commanded, as he pushed his mate out of the line towards the girl. 'That Danny was about as subtle as a sledge-hammer,' Steven thought to himself with a grimace as he found himself staring straight into Tracey's big blue eyes. He smiled awkwardly.

'Danny's a great mate, but just a bit pushy at times,' he said, feeling embarrassed.

'You're lucky to have such a good friend,' Tracey replied with a smile. Then, there was a long pause. Steven just stood there like a store dummy.

'So, Steve,' Tracey began, breaking the

silence, 'I'm really glad I ran into you here. I've felt so rotten about what happened the other day. I didn't mean to put you down like that when you asked me out!' she exclaimed.

'Don't worry about it,' Steven said with a shrug, trying to keep his composure. 'I haven't given it another thought,' he lied.

'But, if I hadn't reacted like such a moron,' Tracey added with sincerity, 'Jock wouldn't have been drawn to investigate and things would never have erupted the way they did. I'm really sorry, Steve,' she whispered with genuine regret.

'Forget it!' Steven exclaimed, as he caught sight of Danny heading over with the tickets.

'Hello people,' Danny said with a taunting smile, as he waved the tickets and indicated that the session was about to start.

'Say do you two mind if I sit with you?' Tracey asked. A smile of ecstasy threatened to break out on Steven's face. But before he could say anything, Tracey continued: 'I hate to sit alone at the movies. I mean, what would people think if they saw me by myself – that I had no friends?' she stammered self-consciously.

127

Steven was stunned by Tracey's comment. Maybe he had bagged her all wrong. She'd always seemed so confident and together. But beneath her 'girl most likely to be popular' exterior, he suddenly realized that Tracey was as vulnerable and insecure as he sometimes felt himself.

Steven and Tracey had a great time together in the movie. They sat with Danny but it was like he wasn't there at all. Steven felt that Tracey and he were on the same wavelength. They laughed at the same gags in the film, even the subtle humour which the rest of the audience seemed to miss. And they whispered together, swapping thoughts and remarks within the darkness, feeling totally at ease in one another's company. Tracey appreciated the fact that she was with someone who treated her like a person, not just a decoration to wear on their arm.

After the show, the trio trailed out of the theatre, clearly happy with the evening's events. But suddenly this happiness evaporated as they were confronted by Jock and a couple of his goon mates who had been waiting in the shadows.

*

'So what's this, Matheson?' Jock accused Steven, as he pointed at Tracey.

'Nothing!' Tracey interrupted defensively.

'I think Matheson and me have a score to settle, Tracey. I'll deal with you later,' Jock replied, by way of diffusing Tracey's intervention.

Steven walked towards Jock, feeling that he was now ready to match with the bully. But Tracey laid a protective hand on Steven's shoulder as she stepped in front of him.

'I'm asking you not to fight, Jock,' she said calmly, looking up into the eyes of the older boy. 'For my sake!' she pleaded.

'I'm ready for the big ape, Tracey,' Steven assured her from behind her back.

'Well, just listen to the little runt!' Jock exclaimed.

'Yeah, and don't we all feel, like, real scared,' added one of Jock's goons as the other one pretended to quiver and shake with fear.

'Cut the sarcasm!' Tracey ordered. 'For heaven's sake, show some maturity. I'm sick to death of things always coming down to an exhibition of physical strength. Fighting! Is that all you lot can do well? So I sat with

Stevie in the movie. You didn't show up, Jock, and it was better than sitting alone,' Tracey snapped, becoming exasperated. She threw Steven a piercing glance. 'You can't think I'd want to be with a little creep like him by choice, can you, Jock?'

Steven's heart crumbled. Jock, on the other hand, rocked with laughter. He linked his arm through Tracey's as Steven felt a pang of jealousy take hold of his inside. Jock's two goons looked confused. But as Jock and Tracey began to walk away, they followed like the sheep they really were.

'Come on, Steve,' Danny said to his stunned mate. 'Forget it! It's over!'

But Steven was fuming. He couldn't believe how Tracey could have changed, just like that.

'Girls!' he shouted in disgust and frustration.

Later, as Steven climbed into the spare bed in Danny's room, he decided that maybe some good could come from what went down with Jock that night.

'Good?' Danny queried. 'How do you figure that?'

'Well I was angry when Jock come up to us

at the theatre,' Steven explained, 'and like my Dad told me this afternoon, no one should fight when they're angry because they're bound to lose.' Steven paused, forming his game-plan. 'I'll take Jock out when I'm calm. And I'll win,' he announced decisively. Danny laughed at this sudden rush of optimism. 'I know you learn karate from your Dad, Steve,' Danny paused, trying to be diplomatic. 'But come on, that Jock Barry is huge. I'm talking "gigantic" here. And no trainee karate kid can match up to someone like that!' Danny added with warning.

'But I'm not just a trainee, Danny,' Steven confided.

'What d'you mean?' Danny asked.

'Well, not that I like to advertise, but I've got my brown belt in karate,' Steven said rather humbly.

Danny flipped. He turned the light back on and looked at Steven, seeming to need to see the truth in his eyes.

'Wow! That's fantastic,' he said with delight. 'I can just see that smug smile being wiped from Jock's face now. I can't wait till you take him out!' Danny shrieked.

'Shh!' Steven whispered. 'This is just between you and me old mate, OK?'

'OK Steve,' Danny promised as he turned out the light. 'But it's OK if I dream about Jock getting what's coming to him, isn't it?'

'Sure,' Steven laughed, as he heard Danny turn over to try to sleep.

Steven looked into the darkness for a time, thinking that Tracey really had cared about what might have happened to him outside the theatre. That's why she'd acted that way; he realized that now! Maybe after he'd taken Jock down a well-deserved peg or two . . . who could say what might happen with Tracey.

As Steven's eyes slowly closed and he began to sink into a deep slumber, he had no idea that across the street, an electrical short circuit was taking place that would change his life forever.

chapter four

From the depths of a wonderful dream, Steven was suddenly awoken by the piercing sound of a siren.

'What's that noise?' Danny growled, drowsily.

'Dunno,' Steven answered as he got out of bed and peered through the window. But what he saw shocked him so absolutely that he stood momentarily frozen.

'Well?' Danny questioned.

'Our house ... our house!' Steven stammered as his heart began to throb rapidly. 'Our house is on fire!' he finally blurted out with horror.

Danny ran to the window. The fire had already engulfed the ground floor of Steven's house.

'I'll get Mum and Dad,' he yelled as he rushed from the room.

Steven felt so helpless as he stood alone, still staring across at his house. Then he saw his mother and father at the window on the top floor. He pulled open Danny's window.

'Mum! Dad!' he called. But no one heard him above the gathering frenzy of the fire trucks below. He watched as his parents desperately tried to dislodge the security grilles, newly fitted to their window. 'They look like prisoners trying to escape' he thought, as the horror of the irony broke upon him. 'Help them, somebody. Help them, please,' he screamed. Then, with Danny and his family following, Steven ran downstairs and out into the street.

'Help my parents,' he yelled again, as he pointed to the figures still struggling with the grilles of the upstairs window.

The firemen gathered the ladder and headed up to the window where the two frantic people were still trapped. The task of cutting the iron grille was an arduous one and Steven could see the fire gaining momentum. 'Hurry,' he called from below. Then he heard a noise like a loud clap of thunder. He saw his father hug his mother to him. And then helplessly he watched as the entire top floor of the house gave way and his parents both plunged to their deaths in the ground floor inferno. It all looked like a slow motion movie. 'No!' he heard himself scream as his own voice echoed in his head. He dropped to the ground, a mangled heap of misery. 'No! No!' he repeated as he beat the ground with his fist.

Danny's mum was beside him, crying and grabbing him to her.

'We're here for you, Steven. Don't worry son,' she sobbed

'My God, I can't believe it, I'm so sorry,' Danny's dad consoled, as he too placed a comforting arm around the boy. Danny stood by, with tears running down his cheeks, unable to speak or move.

The whole thing was over within an hour and by the next morning all that was left of Steven's previous life was the smouldering heap of rubble across the street, the place that he'd once called 'home'.

Steven moved almost zombie-like through the following week. Interviews with the newspapers and TV crews, the funeral, the discussions regarding his future all just seemed a blur of unreality. 'I just can't believe it happened,' Steven kept saying to anyone who was around. 'I keep hoping I'll wake up and it will all have just been a nightmare.'

His Uncle Philip shared his grief; as did Bill, his father's partner at the karate school.

'And just when things were really coming good for us,' Bill said with deep regret. 'Brett didn't deserve this and neither did Alice. Such a damned waste of such damned fine people!'

Philip talked with Steven hour after hour, day after day. But his 'wise uncle' image was often shattered as he broke down during these times and felt unable to cope with the tragedy. Steven, on the other hand, hadn't yet shed a tear. 'Dad wouldn't have wanted me to,' Steven insisted when a concerned Philip confronted him with the fact.

'You've got to let it out, Steve,' Philip advised. 'Otherwise, it's like a fester that will eat away at your insides until it explodes.'

But instead, Steven retreated to the cleansing and purifying of his daily centreing sessions in the park. The movements of fluidity and grace enabled him to control the shrieking grief inside himself.

And Steven's problems extended beyond his personal grief over the loss of his parents, as his own future was something that also played upon his mind. Without his mum and dad, Philip was his only relative. But Philip was doing his residency at one of the major city hospitals and even Steven knew that there was no place in his uncle's life for a teenage boy. While he could stay with Danny's parents temporarily, this, he realised, was only a stop-gap measure.

'I think the Department of Youth and Community Services will have to be brought in, Philip,' Steven overheard Bill telling his uncle when they both thought he was upstairs and out of earshot.

'What? You mean make Steven a foster child?' he heard Philip's voice question.

'It's the only way, mate,' Bill replied, appealing to Philip's rational nature.

Back upstairs in Danny's room, Steven shrank back into himself. The term 'foster child' rang in his head as he sat on the edge of his bed. To Steven it was a label that meant 'unwanted and unloved'. He suddenly felt totally lost and alone; abandoned by everyone in life he had ever felt close to.

His head fell into his hands and his misery rose into his throat as choking tears threatened to break through. 'No!' he commanded himself aloud, as his steel will stepped in and took control once more. All he could do was to head for the park and another session of his centreing exercises.

About three weeks after the night that had changed his life forever, Steven returned to school. Tracey was the first one to seek him out to offer her condolences.

'I can't tell you how sorry I am, Steve,' the girl said tenderly as she sat talking with him in one of the school's alcoves. 'I'll help you to get through this any way I can,' she assured Steven with genuine sincerity.

'Thanks,' he replied, although he knew deep down that no one could really help him.

But suddenly, the solitude of the moment was fractured as Jock Barry came upon the pair and Steven recognized the rage in the older boy's eyes.

'Well, well! So you're back, Matheson,' Jock said with sarcasm. Steven nodded, and glanced away. Jock was definitely not what he needed right now.

'Just cos your folks were barbecued recently,' Jock snarled, as he glared at Steven, 'don't think I'm gonna let you get away with hitting on my girl, like this. Just keep clear of Tracey, or I'll cream you Matheson; understand?' he threatened, as he grabbed Tracey by the arm and pulled her up off the seat.

Something inside Steven suddenly snapped. He sprang to his feet, gritting his teeth in rage.

'You callous, overbearing moron!' Steven spat the words at Jock. 'How dare you even mention my parents!' he screamed with rage as he hurled himself towards the larger boy. But Steven attacked in anger and suffered the consequences. Jock floored him with one powerful king hit which knocked the smaller boy unconscious.

The next thing he knew, Steven was coming to in the school infirmary.

'He's coming round now, Mr Wyndham,' the nurse said as Steven caught sight of the school principal hovering over him.

'OK. Sit up slowly, son,' Mr Wyndham instructed. But Steven noticed a tone of irritation mingled with the caring concern of the principal's voice.

'I'm disappointed in your behaviour, Steven,' Mr Wyndham began, as Steven sat stunned by the fact he was to receive a lecture instead of sympathy. 'I've been informed by some of the witnesses present at the incident that you just seemed to explode with rage and that you seized upon Jock Barry who was merely an unsuspecting passerby at the time.'

'Misinformed,' Steven murmured under his breath, realizing that an argument would only fall on deaf ears.

'Now I know you have been through a terrible trauma,' continued the principal, 'and we all sympathize most deeply with your loss. But you can't allow this tragedy to change you, Steven,' he added as he helped the boy out of the room. 'I want you to maintain the high standards you have always set yourself. You owe it to the memory of your fine parents to continue on your path of academic success.'

Steven quietly nodded. Anything that he could say at this stage would only prolong the principal's oratory.

He waded through the rest of the day at school, keeping mostly to himself. The teachers all seemed understanding but distant. And most of his classmates gave him a wide berth. He'd heard about how people were sometimes shunned by friends when tragedy arose in their lives, now he was experiencing the truth of the tale. Only Danny had really stuck by him over the weeks. But Danny went to another school and even he was away right now on a two-week school camp.

Steven left school that afternoon, feeling as though he didn't have a friend in the world. But, as he rounded the corner to cut through the park, he found Tracey waiting for him.

'How are you feeling?' she asked, sheepishly.

'How'd you think!' he replied a little curtly.

'I feel like a real heel,' she admitted. 'I really wanted to stick up for you when Jock and his mates were telling that pack of lies to the principal but,' she paused, 'the fact is I was just too scared of what Jock might do to me if I went against him!'

Steven felt a twinge of sympathy for Tracey. She was just as intimidated by Jock as the rest of the school was; he understood that.

'Yeh,' he said, 'I know.'

Tracey smiled as she took Steven's hand. 'Sorry! Can you forgive me?' she asked.

'I'll try,' he smiled. 'Come for a walk and we'll talk about it.'

The pair wandered down to the bank of the river that ran through the centre of the park. They sat down on the edge and stared into the running water, drinking in the peace and harmony of Nature.

Then Steven began to talk. He confided all his inner feelings of guilt and insecurity to Tracey. He held nothing back. And as he explained to her the horror of his parents' deaths, he also told her of his own deep grief.

'I feel lost and alone now,' he murmured. 'There is no one I can turn to and it hurts ... it hurts so much,' he added as he suddenly began to sob uncontrollably. Tracey looked away, momentarily embarrassed by the sight of the boy crying.

'I'm sorry, Tracey,' he snivelled. 'I've never cried since it all happened. I guess it's all just overpowered me,' he added, trying to wipe away the persistent tears.

Tracey looked at Steven and her heart

melted. She gathered him into her arms, and he continued to cry out all his frustration while she comforted him.

And as they sat intertwined in each other's arms, each felt that a strong and impenetrable bond had formed between them.

chapter five

During the days that followed, Steven began to gain a new vision of life. Like his Uncle Phil had said, he had needed to let out all the grief that was eating away at him in order for his life to continue. He began to think clearly for the first time since the tragedy had happened. His parents' deaths, he decided, were indirectly caused by the person, or persons, burglarizing the district. If it hadn't been for the neighbourhood robberies, security grilles would never have been needed on the windows of his house, and his mother and father would have been able to leap to safety and would still be alive.

He'd enquired at the police station as to the progress of their investigation regarding the robbers but there had been no further leads. 'We're still working on the theory of a well-organized youth gang,' the desk sergeant had informed Steven, eyeing him a little suspiciously. 'But you keep out of it, kid,' he warned. 'These gangs can get a little rough at times.' Steven nodded, but as he left the police station, his mind was already alive with ideas of how he could help accelerate justice.

'If I get in with the rougher element at school,' he later explained to Tracey, 'maybe I can infiltrate the gang and expose them before a foster home is found for me and I have to leave the district.'

'But Steve, you don't have to do this. Leave it to the police,' she counselled. 'Your parents would never have expected this of you,' she wisely added. But Steven wasn't listening.

'First,' he announced to Tracey, 'I have to establish a "tough-guy" reputation in the playground.'

'No you don't!' she argued, still trying to sway Steven from his plan.

'Yes I do,' he reiterated. 'And I know just how to go about it!' he exclaimed, as a smile of cunning broke on his face.

The next day Steven put his plan into operation.

'Step One,' he said to himself quietly as he

spotted Jock Barry in the playground. 'Annihilation of the bully!' he murmured under his breath.

Calmly, Steven headed towards Jock and his goons.

'Hey Jock,' he called. 'Beat up on any little kids, lately? Or are you targeting girls these days?' he asked, loud enough to gain the attention of just about everyone in the playground. Jock flew into a temper almost immediately.

'So it's Matheson the Mouth, is it?' Jock quipped as he fronted Steven.

'You're a joke to everyone at school,' Steven continued tauntingly, as he looked the older boy directly in the eye. 'Behind your back, even your own mates laugh at you,' he announced. A muffled snigger dominoed through the group of gathered figures which now encircled the pair. As Steven planned, Jock's rage was ignited. He lunged at Steven. But Steven maintained his cool, and effectively enlisted his karate skills to cream the school bully well and truly. Jock landed in a groaning heap on the concrete, shock and amazement written all over his face. The playground suddenly erupted into cheers of delight from the many others who

had suffered at the hands of Jock Barry.
'Good on ya, Stevo!' came the cry from the
exhuberant bystanders. Steven smiled. But
then he remembered the 'tough guy' image
he was seeking to build.

'Anyone else?' he asked, as he stared at
Jock's goons. But soon, it wasn't the goons
he was facing, but Mr Wyndham as he was
sent to the office by one of the teachers who
had intervened in the playground ruckus.

'So Steven, I thought we'd straightened
things out last week?' Mr Wyndham
remarked.

'Well, that was last week!' Steven snapped
back. 'Things have changed.'

'I don't like your attitude here, Matheson,'
the Principal exclaimed. But Steven merely
shrugged.

'You leave me no recourse but to give you
three afternoon detentions. And I must point
out that this penalty is more for your inso-
lence than your fighting. Should there be a
recurrence of this sort of behaviour, the
penalty will be stiffer next time,' Mr Wyndham warned as he dismissed Steven.

As the following weeks plodded by, Steven

watched with pleasure as more and more pieces of his plan fell into place. He stopped wearing his school uniform as a sign of his rebellion, he carried on in a disruptive manner and feigned a lack of attention in all his subjects. As a result his teachers all duly noted his lagging interest and his raucous behaviour and he reinforced their views by his poor showings in class tests.

'You're really blowing things for yourself academically, Steve,' Tracey warned with concern, as they walked home from school together one afternoon. Tracey was now Steven's girlfriend and she genuinely cared about his welfare.

'Look, Trace, once I get dropped into those lower classes and make in-roads with that gang that I suspect of being, or at least knowing, the criminals,' Steven paused, 'well after things clear up, I can make my way back up the academic ladder.'

'But it might not be just that easy!' Tracey said with a snap of her fingers.

'Come on, you don't think I'm flunking these tests for real, do you?' Steven asked her with an affectionate hug. Tracey looked at him questioningly.

'I'm keeping up by studying at night,' Steven explained. 'And then I'm deliberately failing the tests. I could have romped in on any of them, if I'd wanted to!'

Tracey seemed relieved by this information, although she still was a long way from being convinced that Steven should be carrying out his own investigation of the case.

By the end of the week, Steven had in fact been demoted to a lower class 'as a result of both your behaviour and your academic slide', the principal had explained to him. He was secretly delighted by the prospect of being placed in the orbit of the boys he thought would lead him to the burglars. But almost from the first class, Steven was forced to re-evaluate his preconceived belief that only the less intelligent kids would be law breakers. This was a middle-class attitude which had led him astray. In the class in which he was placed, Steven found a wisdom and maturity which had nothing at all to do with academic standing. The group, by whom he was readily accepted, was a raucous and fun-loving bunch, led by an athletic-looking boy by the name of Pete Booker. During lessons, Pete was a rough, tough troublemaker: a handful for any teacher to try to control. But out of the classroom, Steven found Pete to be basically a good-natured type who was loyal to his friends and only concerned that everybody be having 'a good time'. Steven wasted no time in proposing to Pete and the group the plan of his own 'good time'.

'The way I see it, Pete,' Steven urged, as his eyes surveyed the circle of faces which surrounded him, 'a really top time would be to pull off the perfect crime; a crime with a touch of intelligent ingenuity. What d'ya say?' he asked. But the reaction from Pete Booker was not the one Steven had expected.

'Don't screw yourself up, Steven,' Pete counselled. 'You've got something going for you. Sure ... you've hit a bit of a slump right now. But ... you'll pull yourself up again. You don't have to be like us. Get your act back together and go places!' he advised.

Steven was floored as he realized the extent to which he'd misjudged, not only the situation, but the kids assembled around him. There hadn't been a single heckle during Pete's remarks. Steven knew for certain he hadn't found the criminals he was looking for. But as he looked into the street-wise eyes of Pete, he also knew for certain that he had found a new group of friends and a new understanding of people. The learning process extended far beyond the school classroom.

Steven returned to his locker harbouring a mixture of feelings. He was glad about Pete; he'd liked him and his crowd from the moment he'd joined the class. But, on the other hand, he was now no closer to finding the gang of thieves than he had been weeks ago. He'd hit a brick wall and he didn't know where to go. He reached into his pocket for his locker key. It was then that he noticed the folded piece of paper wedged into his locker door.

'OK MR CRIMINAL,' he read, 'YOU WANT TO DO A BIG BUST. DO IT WITH US. MEET YOU DOWN AT THE OVAL AT NINE TONIGHT.'

A smile of fulfilment broke over Steven's face. 'They've taken the bait,' he thought to himself, his mind already racing forward to who he might find waiting for him at the oval that night!

chapter six

Steven arrived back at the Graham's house that afternoon to find Mr Pierce from Youth and Community Services waiting for him.

'I've been concerned to hear about your changing attitude towards school, Steven,' Pierce explained, 'so, I've accelerated the fostering process. I've found a couple who can take you almost immediately,' he added, pausing as he sensed Steven's apprehension at this prospect. 'Come on, Steve, you knew it had to happen sooner or later,' Pierce consoled. Steven shrugged sombrely.

'Tom and Pippa Fletcher are the couple,' Pierce continued. 'Theirs is a big family – a boy and three girls: Frank, Carly, Lynn and Sally. I'm sure that the warm and happy environment they can provide is just what you need, Steve. Get you away from all the tragic memories and they'll have you back on the right track in no time,' he assured Steven, as he placed a caring hand upon his shoulder.

But all Steven could think of was that this could mess up all his plans. He was so close to cracking the case and nabbing those whom he saw as responsible for his parents' deaths, now just wasn't the time to be taken from the district and fostered out.

'I know I have to go,' Steven said to the social worker, 'but please, Mr Pierce, let me have another week. I just need to wind things up here!'

'Well, the thing is, Steve, I don't think I can swing it for you,' Pierce explained. 'You see, Danny's parents feel it's time that you moved on. They have no complaints about your behaviour at home but,' he paused, trying to be as diplomatic as possible, 'but they have been informed by the school of your unruly behaviour and falling grades. Naturally, they're concerned that Danny may be effected. You two have always been so close!'

'But, if I can get them to agree?' Steven asked. 'Can I have another week here, then?' he begged.

Tarquin Pierce looked at the pleading boy and his heart softened.

'If the Grahams agree, I guess I can hold off

another week,' he confirmed. 'But only if the Grahams agree!' he stipulated.

Steven confronted Danny's parents as soon as Mr Graham arrived home that night. He pleaded his case, begging for just a further week to try to patch up his academic record, among other things. The Grahams were reluctant but their kind-hearted natures overcame their anguish. Finally they agreed with Steven's request. And it was a grateful and relieved Steven Matheson who retreated to Danny's bedroom to form his own plan for a meeting scheduled for later that night.

At precisely nine o'clock, Steven walked out on to the school oval and stood just within the range of the one overhead light which illuminated the playing field.

'Hey Matheson!' a muffled voice called from somewhere in the shadows to his right. He turned and headed in the direction of the voice and came upon four tall figures dressed in ragged clothing and wearing balaclavas which concealed their faces. Judging by their size, Steven estimated that these would have to be at least year ten boys. But Steven swallowed hard on the ripple of fear that threatened to overcome his composure. It took no time for him to realize that the group were disguising their voices in a further effort to conceal their identities. And the whole deal wasn't going to be as easy as he had first thought: Steven was to be tested, according to the spokesperson for the group.

'Before we talk turkey with you, Matheson, you've gotta prove you're trustworthy,' the anonymous speaker informed him.

'I am,' he assured them, with as much conviction as he could muster.

'Well, put your talents where you mouth is. You go pull a job now and bring us back the loot. Then we'll know you're really one of us,' the speaker instructed.

'You mean rob a place right now!' Steven said, trying to keep his cool exterior. The group nodded. This was something Steven hadn't counted upon and he was a little rattled.

'OK,' he added as calmly as he could. 'I'll be back in no time!'

Steven's mind was spinning as he left the oval. Of course he couldn't actually rob a house, that was unthinkable! But somehow, he had to prove himself in order to infiltrate the gang. Then he had a brainstorm. He headed for his Uncle Philip's apartment and kept his fingers crossed.

Philip was entertaining female company and wasn't too thrilled with the timing of Steven's visit.

'I just need to borrow your TV and video,' Steven explained. 'And then I'm out of here.'

'Borrow my . . .' Philip began.

'Please Uncle Phil?' Steven interrupted. 'You'll get them back. But I really really need them. It's what you might call an emergency. It's not for money or anything like that, I promise!' he assured his stunned Uncle.

Philip looked at his nephew: he was a good kid; he trusted him. Obviously this was something very important to Steven and the boy had been through a hell of a lot lately.

'I must need my head read,' Philip said. 'But OK! Take them! Take them! Quickly before I change my mind!' he advised.

'Thanks!' Steven gratefully replied as he hastily gathered the compact TV and video in his arms. 'There was no one else on earth like Philip,' he thought to himself as he made his way back to the oval.

As Steven produced the loot to the gang back at the oval, he explained that he had 'borrowed' the stuff from a place nearby. The group all laughed at his use of the term 'borrowed'. Of course they didn't realize the truth of Steven's words. Clearly, Steven had passed the test. The spokesperson for the group stepped into the light. The guy was huge.

'You're a bright one, Matheson, I'll give you that!' the boy mumbled from behind his balaclava. 'You're still a creep but you are bright,' he repeated, as Steven stood looking up at the masked face, sensing something vaguely familiar. 'And maybe with your brains,' the speaker continued, 'we can move on to bigger and better jobs!' The group all nodded their approval of this remark. And Steven found his hand being grasped firmly by the unidentified leader of the gang. 'But any betrayal, Matheson,' came the warning, still in a muffled voice, 'and you're dead meat, if you get my drift! But you're one of us now, so we don't need our disguises any more,' he added as, one by one, the boys removed their headgear.

Steven looked around him at the faces which were gradually being revealed and suddenly he had to muffle his own gasp of dismay as he recognized the leader of the gang as none other than Jock Barry himself!

chapter seven

As dawn broke four days later, Steven woke up with a jolt. He was now used to broken sleep and early mornings as dreams about his parents haunted his nights. But this was the day of the big bust! The day when those indirectly responsible for his parents' deaths should get just what they deserved. He looked across at the still sleeping Danny. He was glad he hadn't involved his mate. It had made things far less complicated.

Steven had worked out an elaborate plan for breaking into the school and ripping off all the computers and electrical equipment. The plan called for him, with his knowledge of electronics, to turn off the alarm system. Then, at the pre-arranged signal, the gang was to go in and start lugging away the merchandise. Jock's group had jumped at the idea. The haul from the school would net them thousands, maybe even hundreds of thousands of dollars. But only Tracey knew of the rest of Steven's plan. And with her help, it wasn't dollars but the gang themselves that would be netted!

Under the cover of darkness that night, the plan went into action!

Unknown to Jock and his group, Tracey stood watch down the street from the school, using a walkie-talkie which Steven had ingeniously connected to a discreet ear-piece receiver which he wore.

Once the alarm had been disconnected and the gang were inside the school, Steven merely phoned the local police. Putting on the voice of a nearby resident, he claimed that he had seen suspicious movements around the school and requested that they investigate. It was then Tracey's job to warn Steven of their approach so he could time the second part of his plan to perfection.

While Jock and company were greedily gathering the school equipment together, Steven rapidly adapted the circuitry of the disconnected alarm so that he could trigger it at will with a transmitting device he carried in his pocket. Then, feigning enthusiasm, he moved in to join the group of looters, who were still engrossed at the assembly of their booty.

'Wow, Matheson! I never thought we'd be into big stuff, like this!' one of Jock's goons commented with delight, as he added another computer to the pile of terminals and monitors stacked in the foyer.

'OK, you lot,' Jock ordered, 'start stashing this lot in the truck.'

'What about old Wyndham's office?' Steven asked, playing for time, as he waited on Tracey's signal.

'It's dead-locked!' Jock said with a shrug. 'Anyway, we've got heaps!'

'Come on,' Steven urged. 'We haven't come this far to leave anything behind, have we? I know where the secretary keeps her spare key,' he added, as he led Jock and one of his goons down the dim corridor by the beam of his flashlight. Steven unlocked the Principal's door and Jock and the other boy seized on Mr Wyndham's own terminal and monitor. 'And go through his desk!' Jock ordered. 'You never know what personals the old bloke might keep at work,' he added with greed written all over his face.

Steven flashed his torchlight round the office,

thinking how else he could play for time. If the police didn't arrive soon, the whole gang would get away with all this stuff, and his own plan would fall flat on its face. He began to feel an anxiety rising from the pit of his stomach.

'I think that's it, Matheson,' Jock said, looking satisfied. 'Just help us load up the last of what's stacked in the foyer and we can take off.'

'OK,' Steven agreed with a gulp. But then he heard Tracey's sweet voice in his ear.

'They're on their way, Steve. I hope you can hear me. The police are just coming up to the school gates now,' she whispered over the walkie-talkie.

Steven wasted no time in activating the transmitter in his pocket. And suddenly, the school's alarm system sang out its ear piercing shriek.

Jock's face went ashen. In sheer panic, he left what was lying on the foyer floor and ran towards the truck, not even glancing back at Steven.

'Gun it!' he screamed as he climbed in.

'What about Matheson?' one of the goons queried.

'Forget him!' Jock yelled. The truck roared away from the building and headed towards the front gates, right into the arms of the approaching police.

Steven walked calmly across the oval and jumped over the school's back fence to join Tracey at her vantage point down the street.

'Success!' he announced jubilantly as they hugged and congratulated each other. Steven had achieved exactly what he had set out to do. The gang had been arrested in the act, with the loot, and without the least suspicion on their part that Steven had betrayed them.

'Jock and his boys are well and truly hooked, Tracey,' Steven confirmed with pride.

'And you're free,' Tracey added with happiness. 'Even if Jock tried to incriminate you, who'd believe him? Everyone knows that you two are mortal enemies!' she laughed, appreciating the ingenuity of Steven's plan.

A police follow-up on the arrest unearthed a cache of booty previously taken by the gang. Philip was stunned when his TV and video were returned to him by the police instead of by Steven. He knew Steven had been up to

something but the grinning school boy
refused to spill the beans. And his uncle was
smart enough not to drop any bombshells to
the police himself.

Finally, the day of Steven's departure to join
his new family arrived. Steven realized that
he still had a long way to go before he could
feel his life was together again. But, although
he was still troubled by dreams of his
parents' deaths, at least his actions in bring-
ing the street gang to justice had helped him
greatly in starting on a new path.

In the park, he centred himself and felt somehow that his father knew of what had trans-
pired and approved. It was funny, but that
closeness, that bond he had felt with his father
on that last afternoon, had never faded. Even
death hadn't been able to diminish it. Steven
took comfort from this feeling as he made his
way back to Danny's house for the last time.

Inside, Tarquin Pierce waited for him. As did
all the friends he had made during his search
for justice. Steven looked around the room
at the group assembled before him. Apart
from Mr Pierce and the Grahams, Pete
Booker and the gang and Tracey had all
come to see him off.

'See ya, Steve!' Pete said as he and his friends rumbled playfully with Steven. 'And remember, you're goin' places for all of us too,' he added with a wink.

'You bet!' Steven assured him.

'We wish you every happiness, son,' Mr and Mrs Graham added, as Mrs Graham gave her 'favourite neighbour' a goodbye hug.

'And don't forget to come back and visit,' Danny urged a little sadly.

'Now, Danny. How could I ever forget my best mate!' Steven exclaimed. 'We've still got to go up Scaler's River to get into those giant bream, haven't we?' he added with a smile.

'Whenever you're ready,' Danny replied enthusiastically. 'I'll be there!' he continued with a grin.

'You're on!' Steven exclaimed, as he and his mate did their own special version of a handshake.

'And what about me?' Tracey queried. 'Will you come back to see me too?' she asked, as Pete and his gang began a few ribbing 'yahoos' and whistles in the background.

'Hey, we're a team, Tracey,' Steven announced. And then he whispered to her: 'The police might need our help again on their next case!'

Tracey giggled, enjoying their own private joke.

'I'll never forget you, Steve,' she promised as she hugged him. 'You made me realize that looks aren't everything. What really counts is what's going on inside your head. You've helped me to grow up and become a decent human being,' she added proudly.

Steven kissed her gently. He didn't care what anyone thought. Tracey had helped him to grow up as well.

As he drove away with Mr Pierce, he waved back to all his friends until the car turned the corner and he could see them no more. Inside himself, Steven felt that he had also just turned a corner in his own life; although he would never forget this time and the friends he had just left behind.

In no time, it seemed, Mr Pierce was parking the car outside an inner city terrace. A pleasant looking couple emerged from the house, followed by four smiling kids ranging in age from nineteen to eight. And Steven had a gut feeling that, just as his new friends back home had started him on the road to adulthood, these six people he now looked at would continue taking him there.

Suddenly, he was filled with hope and anticipation. From here, he decided to himself, his future would begin!

**OTHER BOOKS FROM
FANTAIL**

FANTAIL

THE HOME AND AWAY SERIES

The **Home And Away** TV show is one of the most successful soaps ever to hit the screens and, as prequels to the gripping television saga, the following books tell the stories of your favourite characters prior to the TV series.

The Matt Wilson Story   0140 90154X

Matt Wilson is the ultra-cool surfing hero of Summer Bay. Strong and tanned, his good looks become the focus for many a teenage schoolgirl crush. But Matt is to find that although admiring fans flatter his ego with all the attention they pay him, they are quite unable to support him through times of disappointment and heartache.

The Bobby Simpson Story   0140 901272

Bobby Simpson, having been deserted by her real mother, is brought up by parents she believes are her own. Forced to suffer rough treatment at the hands of her adoptive father and being victimised by the deputy head of her school makes Bobby rebel in the only way she can. Bobby is to grow from being a wild tomboy to a deeply troubled young woman yearning for security and love.

The Frank Morgan Story   0140 901280

Frank Morgan's father is a criminal, his mother an alcoholic and Frank is running wild. At the age of 8 he tries to prove himself to his father by robbing a bank. But the police catch up with the boy and he is taken away from home and sent into care. The Fletcher family try hard to make Frank's life a happier one but unfortunately his troubles are not destined to end so soon.

Mr Majeika's Magical TV Fun Book 0140 901961

Mr Majeika is back again with stories, jokes, recipes and games to play with your friends. Follow the antics of your favourite wizard from Walpurgis as he helps to save a family of foxes, narrowly escapes having to marry an ugly mermaid and clambers over icy rooftops to lend Santa a hand in three spellbinding adventures.

Skateboarding Is Not A Book   0140 900349

Whether you are a novice "street" skater or a highly paid
professional skateboarding star this book is for you.
Skateboarding is an obsession and a way of life for millions of
people all over the world – and it's GROWING. Skateboarding
Is Not A Book covers everything you need to know about the
sport – its history, the equipment you need and where to find it,
where to skate, injuries and those crucial skills and techniques.